LETHAL RED SECRETS
A MIA TREADWELL STORY

G.K. LAWRENCE

© **Copyright 2022 - All rights reserved.**

The content contained within this book may not be reproduced, duplicated or transmitted without direct written permission from the author or the publisher.

Under no circumstances will any blame or legal responsibility be held against the publisher, or author, for any damages, reparation, or monetary loss due to the information contained within this book, either directly or indirectly.

Legal Notice:

This book is copyright protected. It is only for personal use. You cannot amend, distribute, sell, use, quote or paraphrase any part, or the content within this book, without the consent of the author or publisher.

Disclaimer Notice:

Please note the information contained within this document is for educational and entertainment purposes only. All effort has been executed to present accurate, up to date, reliable, complete information. No warranties of any kind are declared or implied. Readers acknowledge that the author is not engaged in the rendering of legal, financial, medical or professional advice. The content within this book has been derived from various sources. Please consult a licensed professional before attempting any techniques outlined in this book.

By reading this document, the reader agrees that under no circumstances is the author responsible for any losses, direct or indirect, that are incurred as a result of the use of the information contained within this document, including, but not limited to, errors, omissions, or inaccuracies.

PROLOGUE
1967

The young man adjusted his green cap to keep the morning sun, sparkling off the water on the Liaodong Bay, out of his eyes. The terrain was flat out there and he could see—for the first time—the vastness of his homeland. Small patches of snow clung for life in the autumn climate and tan grass poked out here and there where the snow was gone. The decommissioned Soviet truck he drove rocked back and forth, bouncing with every slight imperfection in the dirt road. A gift from the Warsaw pact, the second-hand junk was retired by their northern neighbors and comrades, but not the new ones with the shocks still intact. He checked the rearview mirror. The wooden trailer hitched behind him jostled around and the young man tried to stay slow so it wouldn't roll and snap the hitch.

Everything about his appearance and demeanor was military. Minimal. Functional. But for one thing. He caught sight of a wetland with red plants, so large it extended past the horizon. A strange phenomenon, unlike anything he'd ever seen. It was almost alien, like looking over the landscape of Mars. The Revolution rejected superstitions and supernatural explanations, but he couldn't help but feel this was a sign. He picked some and decorated the truck a bit with the red plants, winding it around the bolts of the vehicle's frame. Despite his paramilitary role, the color seemed appropriate and forgivable.

He stopped and unfolded his map. There was hardly a feature in these plains to get his bearings with, and the names of many places had been crossed out and replaced with new names, better names. He blew hot breath into his hands and rubbed them together before pressing them to his ears, which were pink and tingling. Without any trees or mountains or buildings to block it, the wind whaled hard on him and stole every bit of warmth. He didn't need it. The Revolution kept him warm.

He continued along the road, stopping once to refill the gas from a can in the back. When he found the village, he didn't need to ask to make sure he was in the right place. The streets were packed with every single person in the community. They crowded the main dirt thoroughfare, yelling and shaking their fists and cursing, maybe 200 of them, and they parted for the truck as he drove through. He parked in the middle of the road, killing the engine when he reached the source of the mob's anger.

He saw five people on their knees, faces looking down in shame at the cold dirt. They all wore tall, white pointed dunce hats, a third as tall as they were. They didn't argue. They didn't disagree. They shamefully absorbed the abuse of their neighbors, friends, and family, who called them the worst names anyone could be called. Words that were accusations—and accusations were death sentences. Bourgeois. Reactionary. Capitalist. Counter-revolutionary. Greedy.

He wasn't there for those people. The young man heeded the call of Mao Zedong, just the same as all Red Guard. He was here as Mao's paramilitary youth, the social enforcement wing, delivered with the passion and energy only possessed by the young. They were there to destroy the old so something new and better could be built. They were there to destroy the Four Olds: Old Ideas, Old Culture, Old Customs, Old Habits. His mission here was specifically the Old Culture.

Three others from the village wore the same uniform he did. They raised fists to greet him. Teenagers, all armed with more Soviet gifts: AK-47s. They didn't respect the Old Custom of respecting their elders. The mob was incited by them, grown adults, most of them more than twice their age, yielding and obeying the youth, asking them what to do, how to behave. These teenagers were here to punish their neighbors and make everyone in the village participate or to accuse the reluctant of being enemies, too.

The young lady with the tight braids introduced herself, in Mandarin, "I am Zhang Ya Ying! Captain of this brigade!" She was short but she took up a lot of space with her loud voice. The entire brigade was just the three of them, it seemed.

The young man raised a fist back. "Where is it?"

"Come with me!" she commanded. She walked with her back stiff and her chin up. Every step she took was a march.

He followed her into a small house, not much more than a clay hut. Inside the living room, all the meager furniture had been pushed to the walls, making room to expose where the villagers hid a hole, four cubic feet. Inside the hole was art. It wasn't local; it was beyond what these people would ever see in their entire lifetimes. These pieces were smuggled from the wealthy, smuggled from the elites.

The art of the enemy. The art of the past. The art of oppression and ignorance. The young man was here to take it and destroy it before the next generation could be infected with the counter-revolutionary ideology that infiltrated every molecule of it.

"What are we to do, comrade?" asked Captain Zhang.

He looked over the items. A fine painting of the Empress Dowager, Tzu-Hsi. Luxurious robes made of a material softer than anything he'd ever felt, gold patterned and brilliantly colored, the exact opposite of the clothes worn by a member of The Party. A hat, a Qing Guanmao, the object of the office of the last dynasty, before the KMT, before the CCP. Shoes with smaller, fake shoes underneath like stilts, to create the illusion of tiny feet when the real was covered with robes, a way of faking foot binding. Dozens of items that would be tremendously valuable to capitalists and those who still held onto the Old Ideas.

He said, "Load it up into the truck. I'm taking it to Beijing."

"May I ask why?"

"I've been told to bring it to Beijing to be burned in front of others, so they can see the good work we're all doing."

Her harsh face almost smiled. She kept looking at the young man as she barked her orders to the others. "Gather it up!"

The others did as she said. The captain was not above helping, and neither was the young man. He reached in and grabbed the closest object: a wooden box with a deep red lacquer. Delicate carvings on the outside revealed a scene from Chinese folk religion. This box was decorated with images of old fairy tales, back when every word, every idea, and everything in nature had a god. He didn't recognize one character, though: a man in a straw hat, digging canals.

Opening the clasp, he peeked inside and swallowed hard when he saw it. The ferocious, judging eyes of the captain remained fixed on his face as he closed the box and carried it outside.

A girl approached the captain and handed her a camera. She took pictures of their work. She ordered the others to lay a cloth down in front of the prisoners, and they did as she said. She ordered them to place the art on the blanket, and they did as she said. She ordered the prisoners to spit on the art. They all did as she said. The captain took pictures of the youth carrying the items, then took pictures of all of it laid out on the blanket. She took pictures of the ferocious mob and the shamed prisoners. When she exhausted her roll of film, she ordered them to load the truck. Carelessly, they tossed their delicate, priceless items like ordinary trash. But not the young man who brought the truck. He added the box to the truck gently.

When the truck was full, he raised a fist, as did the others. The crowd cheered him and then began kicking dirt and throwing rocks at the five people on their knees. They all understood that the least enthusiastic abuser would be the next person to be suspected of crimes against the revolution, so they all made sure to show exaggerated glee at their cruelty.

It took him a few tries, but he got his truck running. Sometimes it was a fight when it was cold. He drove out through the opposite side of the village, bouncing on the pothole-dimpled road. He flinched when he heard the clatter of revolutionary assault rifles behind him. He didn't need to look. He knew how they were used. He'd seen them used enough and he never needed to look again. The crowd cheered the murder of their neighbors and their Old Habits.

He drove slowly over the bumpy road of frozen mud,

potholed and uneven, far past the village and their farms. Out there, the roads were hardly more than parallel lines in the grass. Spotting the first road sign he'd seen for two days, he checked his map. One arrow pointed to Beijing, the other to Dalian. He pressed the brake and brought the truck to a stop. He looked at those signs for a long time before he decided which road he would take.

CHAPTER
ONE
PRESENT DAY

Mia was under the trance of Debbie Harry's vocals singing "Picture This" as she read the bio of the man she was on her way to meet.

Hau Junjie. Thirty-five-year-old wunderkind, programmer, entrepreneur, and art collector. He started as a computer programmer from a modest, middle-class family. Went to the London School of Economics. Wrote some software and founded Sesame Road, which now runs logistics for almost 90% of the Hong Kong market. SR has also expanded recently into Malaysia, Singapore, and Thailand, and is presently bidding for contracts in Africa. Hau is a fan of film, with several credits as a movie producer.

Mia didn't recognize any of the titles he'd produced. Mostly action movies, by the look of it. The kind of junk Raphael would love.

"Mm? Mmm mm mm?"

Mia removed her earbuds and looked to her right. "I'm sorry, what?"

The boy with messy hair asked, "Did you know that in the event of a nuclear attack, you can protect your electronics from electromagnetic radiation by putting them inside your microwave?"

"No, Raphael. I was not aware of that."

"Microwave ovens block microwaves so you don't cook the whole kitchen, and they also block radio waves."

"What are you reading?" She leaned over to get a glimpse at the tablet her son was holding.

"*Art of War* by Sun Tzu."

"I'm pretty sure he didn't know about radio waves and nuclear weapons."

"I just finished a different book about nuclear war."

"Why do you need to read about stuff like that? It's so grim."

He shrugged.

A flight attendant approached and took their orders.

"Um, I'll have a seltzer, please."

The Asian-American woman to her left said, "Do you have beer? I'd like a Singha, if you have it. Thank you." She had been sleeping the entire flight, gently snoring, and Mia only just noticed she was awake.

The attendant moved on to the next row. The woman reached into her purse and produced a small, beautifully decorated gold and red tin, with the art of a Chinese guardian lion. She opened it up and took out a piece of dried ginger candy, which she popped in her mouth.

"That's funny," said Mia.

"Hm? Are you speaking to me?"

"Oh, no. More to myself. Just a weird coincidence."

"How's that?"

"You ordered a Singha. That's the Khmer word for the lion on your tin."

She looked at the tin. "Lion? No, this is a dog."

"I don't want to be the person who says, 'well, actually,' but..."

"Really? This is a lion? I bought this because I thought it was a dog." She chuckled. "I have three rescues at home."

"They're sometimes called foo dogs, but it's supposed to be a representation of a lion. You usually find them in a male and female pair outside of Buddhist temples. Yours is female."

"How can you tell?"

"She's got a paw on a little cub that's on its back. Males have a ball under their paw."

"Why do they look like dogs then?"

"You have to put yourself in the minds of the artists at their time in history. The artists never saw a lion. They probably never went more than 50 miles away from where they were born, and they didn't have zoos and photographs to work with. They had to go by descriptions other people gave them, probably second-hand, like that children's game telephone. They did their best guess of what a lion looked like. Then other artists just copied the work of their teachers, assuming this must be what a lion looks like. That's how you get a lion that looks like a British bulldog."

"Huh. That's interesting. Are you a Chinese historian?"

"No, actually, my expertise is in Byzantine Orthodox art. I've been trying to learn as much about the subject as I can for my trip."

"We have about three more hours on this flight. At this rate, I expect you'll be an expert before we land." She squinted a little. "I feel like I know you from somewhere. Have we met before?"

"Mm, I don't think so."

"You have a very... distinct appearance. Are you Khmer?"

Mia had heard countless people stumble over those

kinds of words before. When the topic came up, people had to gently navigate unspoken social rules without knowing exactly what the rules even are anymore. Mia understood, though. People often had difficulty figuring out her family's origins, often guessing that she was Maori, half-Black and half-Asian, or some other novel phenotypic cocktail. It was always more awkward for them than it was for Mia. She reflexively smiled to cut the tension.

Mia asked, "Do you like true crime?"

"I do!"

"Do you listen to the Alternative Theories Podcast?"

"Yes, of course, I watch their videos online... Wait, are you...?"

Mia nodded, a little embarrassed.

The woman continued, "You're that lady who found the stolen art in Colorado?"

"That's me."

"That was one of their best episodes! Wow! That story was something else. Those terrible murders... You're kind of a celebrity."

"No, hold on, I don't know about all that."

"Well, you are in the true crime world. That story was all anyone could talk about for weeks. It was nice to have a break from that other infamous case in Colorado... But it's working out, right? You're sitting in first class, so you must be doing well."

"This is actually my first time in first class. A client is paying, so... let's just say that *he* is doing very well."

"It's so much money, but it's amazing what a difference only two extra inches of legroom makes. I'm Xiaoli." She offered a hand.

Mia shook it. "Mia Treadwell. And this is my son, Raphael."

"Hi." He barely looked up from his book.

"You're the son! Oh my goodness! You were there for all of that. Wow. Do you know how cool your mom is?" Xiaoli asked.

Raphael nodded without looking up from his book.

Xiaoli leaned back and said, "I'm absolutely addicted to these candies. I'm on medication that makes things taste weird and the bite of the ginger helps. Would you like one?"

Mia shook her head and held up a hand. They were so strong that Mia could smell them. Xiaoli reached the tin out to Raphael. "How about you?"

He made a face when the aroma of ginger reached him. "No, I'm fine, thanks."

"What kind of work do you have in Hong Kong?"

Mia struggled to answer. "That's the thing. Uh, I don't know quite yet. I was putting off taking a new job for a month. See, we just moved into a new home in Colorado. We weren't even unpacked when I got this offer. The money was so good, how could I say no? I spoke with my client's personal assistant. They were light on the details and they booked me a flight right away. And my son has recently taken an interest in Asian military history, so... here we are. It was very important that they have the meeting in person. I figure the worst-case scenario is I don't take the job, and me and Raphael have a fun week in Hong Kong."

The captain made an announcement that they were beginning their descent. Mia excused herself from the conversation and took a last-minute opportunity to use the restroom. When she got out, Xiaoli was waiting to use it next. Her aisle neighbor had a dreamy look in her eyes. Mia smiled at her, but Xiaoli didn't acknowledge her and didn't even seem to see her. She slipped into the restroom the moment Mia cleared the way.

Mia sat down, buckled up, and told Raphael to do the same. The flight attendants walked up and down the rows to make sure everyone was seated and buckled in. Xiaoli hadn't returned.

An attendant knocked on the door. "Ma'am? The plane is landing. You have to return to your seat. Ma'am?"

After calling for another attendant to help, and further repeated requests, there was still no response. The staff closed a curtain to protect the privacy of the person in the restroom while a key was used to open the door.

"Oh my god!"

The people in first class became very alert at the sound of flight staff saying something like that, especially on the descent. There was some movement and commotion behind the curtain.

"Mom? What's going on?"

"I don't know."

Over the speakers, the flight attendant asked, "Attention, passengers. One of the passengers is experiencing a medical emergency. Are there any doctors on this flight?"

A man sitting behind the Treadwells was already unbuckled and walking to the front before the second sentence. He slipped to the other side of the curtain and started asking questions of the staff and checking her vitals.

Just beneath the one-inch gap under the curtain, Mia could see the doctor knelt and was giving chest compressions to Xiaoli while giving orders to the crew.

"Bring me a defibrillator!"

CHAPTER TWO

It took a while before they were allowed to leave the plane. The curtain remained up. The seat next to Mia remained empty. And the doctor who had volunteered was back in his seat. Paramedics were ready the moment the door opened and they took her away on a gurney, without hurrying.

When Xiaoli's body was removed, the passengers started filing out. Everyone was quieter and more patient than usual. On their way out, people approached Mia and asked her if she knew what happened, and she kept telling them she didn't.

Once they were through customs, they took an escalator downstairs to the luggage carousels. They filed in along with the others Mia recognized from their plane. She overheard pieces in their conversation and many were talking about the poor woman who died. She stared at the conveyor belt hypnotically, snapping out of it when she saw her bag coming down the carousel. She reached a hand out to take it, but another snapped out and caught it before her, removing the heavy bag with ease.

"Um, excuse me?" Mia spoke in a firm but genuinely confused tone.

"Dr. Treadwell?" The man was a little short, his jaw and cheekbones distinct. He must've had barely an ounce of fat on his body. He wore a suit: black pants, a white shirt, a black sports jacket, and a black tie, all just a little baggy. He had nice clothes, but he hardly put any effort into them. He wore it as he disdained it. Sunglasses hung from his neck.

"Yes?"

He extended a hand. "Welcome to Hong Kong. My name is Michael Fong. I'm your driver."

"Driver?" she asked, which felt like a silly question as soon as she said it. "I wasn't expecting that."

"Mr. Hau is very excited to have you here."

She looked at Raphael. His eyebrows went up and he made an exaggerated expression with his mouth, a face that silently said, "Fancy." She made the same face right back at him.

When she took Fong's hand and shook it, Mia noticed his knuckles were scarred up and had a couple fresh scabs.

"Please, call me Mia. And this is Raphael."

"Good to meet you." Raphael shook his hand.

"Oh! Bag!" Mia realized one was getting away from her during their introductions. Mr. Fong grabbed it quickly. He insisted on doing all the lifting of the bags. Despite his small stature, he was very strong.

When he had all four of their bags, he led them through the automatic glass doors to a mint silver Rolls Phantom. The hazard lights were blinking. As he popped the trunk and put their stuff in, the Treadwells climbed into the back, through coach doors.

"Whoa," came out of Raphael's mouth. He reached for the minibar.

Mia gently slapped his hand. "Not on your life."

Fong climbed into the driver's seat.

"This is very fancy. I'm glad no one towed you."

He smiled. "Don't worry, Doctor. They all know not to tow this car. I'm going to take you to your hotel now, if that's alright with you. I know it's been a long flight."

"That would be great, Michael. And you don't have to call me Doctor. Only my colleagues call me that. Or should we call you Mike?"

"Mr. Fong is fine, ma'am."

He took a ramp onto the highway. It was strange adjusting to all the vehicles driving on the opposite side of the road. With plastic barriers, striped walls and reflectors, orange-vested men, yellow machines, and cranes everywhere, it looked like the whole place was under construction. The sun was low, half a lens flare behind the mountains just visible beyond the buildings.

"Is it morning or evening?" asked Raphael.

"It is just about 8 p.m. now."

Even with the sun going down, the grass was so green. Mia had only seen grass like that in Hawaii. The mountains weren't like the Rockies, either. They were so steep and verdant, stabbing into the heavy, fluffy orange and magenta clouds. And the city was right there. Within just a minute, they were surrounded by buildings. She'd never seen an airport so close to civilization. The ride was as smooth as could be, which was a credit to the road management or the vehicle's engineers.

They drove under bridges and over them, the highway system like the tangle of a Celtic knot. Billboards pointed motorists to products Mia had never heard of, and everything was written in Chinese and English. This city loved glass. Most of the buildings they passed—the convention centers, the hotels, and structures bridging the road—had big, reflective walls of glass. All very modern. Everything was open, like the architects wanted to show there was nothing inside of them to hide. There were places where the jungle growth would stealthily, slowly try to take back the island from civilization, places where the trees and vines were poking out of flaws in the concrete, or climbing the buildings and sound barriers and bridges.

"How was the flight, ma'am?"

"Fine, but..." Mia hardly even wanted to say it.

Raphael said, "A lady sitting next to Mom died."

"She died next to you, ma'am?"

"No, she was sitting next to me, but she was... You know, I think I'd rather not talk about it anymore."

"Yes, ma'am."

They crossed under a road sign pointing toward Tsing Yi, Kowloon, and Hong Kong, and over a cable bridge so long it took nearly four minutes to cross, then right into those green mountains, headlong through a long tunnel. They disappeared into the stone passage, through hundreds of feet of rock, and when they came out the other side, it was like waking up from a dream.

Just like those mountains, the skyscrapers appeared abruptly and swallowed the horizon. They were packed so tightly that it became a dense maze of angular geometry, apartments like human hives. The buildings stood like huge monuments to modernity, with occasional glimpses at the sky between them. As the sun disappeared, the lights came on and the sky became black as the streets began to glow. Headlights, signage, and large neon screens like drive-in theaters were as bright and loud as Vegas, but half as garish.

Fong pulled into the drive of a massive hotel and up to

the valet parking in front. Mia looked out, thinking there must be a mistake. The hotel was beyond anything she'd ever stayed at. Fong parked, stepped out, and opened the doors for the Treadwells, while their bags were handed off from the trunk to a man in a suit and white gloves, who carried them away on a red and gold cart.

"It was a pleasure to meet you, ma'am. Raphael. I will let you two get some rest. Your meeting with Mr. Hau is at 10:30 a.m. tomorrow. I will be here at 10. Is there anything else you need before I leave?"

"No, thank you, Mr. Fong. This is so much more than I was expecting. You've been great. Thank you."

"One other thing. You probably haven't eaten dinner yet, and the food here is very good. Everything will be billed to Mr. Hau, naturally."

THE ROOM WAS MORE like a suite. Two king-sized beds, a desk, and a bathroom as nice as any Mia had ever visited, with a shower and a deep jacuzzi. Raphael opened the blinds to see the sparkling electric city, the headlights of vehicles moving through the streets. An amazing view, even without sunlight.

Mia dropped her backpack on the bed and fell onto it backward. It was the most comfortable bed she'd ever felt, or maybe just the most comfortable thing she'd sat on in almost 20 hours.

She asked no one, "How can sitting still for 15 hours be the most exhausting thing in the world?"

"I call first dibs on the shower." Raphael went in and closed the door.

"Knock yourself out," said Mia. She closed her eyes but

she kept seeing Xiaoli on the floor, getting defibrillated. Then, the doctor stood up and returned to his seat with a defeated look in his eyes when there was nothing else he could do. The staff had stuffed her back into the restroom and closed the door, so that her body wouldn't fly around the cabin in the event of an emergency.

The dinner menu was a QR code printed on a piece of paper on the desk. Mia picked up her phone to scan it and connected to the wifi, but the battery was running low. She sat up, opened her backpack, and dug around inside, looking for her charger. Her bag was chaotic. It annoyed Raphael's father, who was always so orderly. Her bag was a mess of objects for every possible situation: wet wipes, spare AA batteries, a bottle of ibuprofen, a small bag of pretzels.

Becoming frustrated, she dumped the contents out onto the bed and spread them around so she could see everything. She found her charger easily but paused when she noticed a stowaway among her personal things.

"How did you get in here?"

She picked it up. Xiaoli's tin with the foo dogs, where she kept her ginger candies. Mia opened it, recoiling at the powerful scent of ginger. The tin had a stowaway of its own. She delicately plucked out a SIM card and held it up.

CHAPTER

THREE

Mia woke up suddenly, confused by the time and place. Jetlag had her all turned around. She looked at the clock to see it was 4:30 a.m. She couldn't sleep. Raphael was still snoring in his bed, but Mia got up, started the tiny coffee pot, and did her ordinary morning routine. She put in her contacts. She dressed in a black T-shirt and acid-wash jeans, and pulled her long black hair into a folded ponytail bun.

She didn't turn on any lights, so as not to bother her son. Using a toothpick from her backpack, she removed the SIM card on her phone, then added the one from Xiaoli's tin and booted it up. She poked around but found nothing. It was blank. A little disappointed, she replaced her SIM card and put Xiaoli's back in the tin, and back into the bag.

RAPHAEL STILL HAD a croissant in his mouth as Mia shooed him through the door, telling him they were going to be late. Downstairs, Fong was waiting, just as he promised. He got out to let them in, but Mia said, "You don't have to do that. We're fine, thank you." And she got in.

Mr. Hau's building wasn't far. With the sun up, she had a better sense of the city. They were in a high-end business district. Most of the people walking were dressed like professionals, or like people who work for professionals. They approached the office building and it was just as Mia imagined it: tall, glass, a mirror reflecting the sky and mountains. Surrounded by a garden, with a pair of bridges from the building across the main road into a parking structure. A big sign out front read: Sesame Road.

The car drove past the visitor and employee parking lots, past the drop-off, and instead approached a metal gate and the bottom of a ramp leading under the building. The gate automatically opened as sensors detected the car and verified who owned it. As they drove down into a private parking lot, the lights automatically switched on.

It was nothing like the dirty, dangerous parking garages Mia was familiar with in New York, where she kept pepper spray close as she speed-walked through. By the looks of the vehicles, only the bigshots parked here. Fong pulled into a reserved spot, cut the engine, and walked around to open the doors for his passengers, but they were out and on their feet before he could get to them.

He led them to a pair of silver doors and waved a card. They opened to reveal a private elevator. They all stepped in. The elevator said something in Chinese, and Fong answered, "Liùshíbā." The elevator seemed to understand him. It started moving, accelerating so quickly that Mia could feel that dropping sensation in her gut. After two floors, the elevator emerged out of the earth. The elevator was glass on all sides. The city shrank beneath them, and Mia quickly realized that the floor was glass, too. She reflexively grabbed the banister and looked up. Her whole body tensed.

"Don't worry, ma'am," said Fong.

"I'm not worried," Mia replied, but her eyes were struggling to look at anything but the floor. "I'm sure it's safe." She said it to herself as much as to the driver.

"I mean, don't worry about being embarrassed. You're doing much better than I did my first time in this thing."

Raphael didn't mind it one bit.

Mia forced herself to look out the sides. The view was unreal. On the ground, the city felt like a maze of impossibly high walls of glass and concrete. It was confusing, and there was no way to see past a couple blocks. At this height, it looked like a model that architects used to use to sell designs. Unconfined. So free she felt like she could fall if she looked down, like in an old cartoon where the coyote runs off the cliff.

The elevator found its destination on the 68th floor. When Fong invited her out with a gesture, she got off, but tried not to get off so fast he'd notice.

The full windows revealed so much of the island. There were hardly any other buildings as tall as this one. A young man behind a desk greeted them in English. Fong nodded and took a seat, leaned back into the deep cushions. There were couches, chairs, and coffee tables, making the waiting room look more like a lounge at a high-end country club.

"You can have a seat, ma'am. Sometimes it takes him a minute."

Mia sat down and the couch was so soft that she sunk deep into it. She was startled when a young woman appeared from seemingly nowhere. "Oh, I'm sorry. I didn't see you there."

The young lady smiled. "Dr. Treadwell. Can I offer you something to drink?"

"A water would be fine." Mia nodded and turned her attention to the driver.

"And for Mr. Treadwell?"

"Me? Um, cappuccino?"

"You're not old enough for coffee," said Mia.

"Ginger ale?"

The woman nodded. "Mr. Fong?"

"Matcha, please."

She smiled and vanished behind a barely visible door, like it could be a secret passageway.

"Mr. Hau is ready to see you now," said the man behind the desk.

"It's okay if my son waits out here?"

"Yes, of course."

Mia and Fong stood up and the driver led her through the oversized double doors into the office.

The room was more like a museum than an office. It held a world-class collection of artifacts that many museums would be jealous to borrow. Tapestries depicted significant events in history that Mia knew very little about. Jade statues stood behind glass cases, along with jars, like urns, bearing elaborate and delicate paintings. A minimalist wooden mannequin wore a dress so immaculate and elaborate, Mia could easily guess the status of the woman who owned it 100 years ago, or longer. She was so enamored with the art she almost forgot to acknowledge her host.

"Dr. Treadwell. Thank you for coming. I'm Hau Junjie."

He looked like his picture. A tall man, clean-cut, in a gray suit made by a well-known Italian designer. His profile said he was in his mid-30s, but he looked like he could be in his 20s. He had the same expression on his face that she'd seen in all of his pictures—an almost smile, like the Mona Lisa. Was it a practiced, polite smile, or was that just how his face naturally was?

He walked around to the front of his desk and extended a hand. She approached it and shook it. His hand was so soft, she might be a little jealous.

"Hi, Mr. Hau. It's good to meet you. This is quite a place you have."

Fong kept to the rear of the room.

"You like my collection?" asked the CEO.

"Yes. Very much. But I'm afraid this isn't my area of expertise."

"Art is for everyone. Not just experts."

She smiled and nodded.

"Which would you say you like most?" he asked.

She surveyed the room. The room was hardly an office at all, save for the desk. It was larger than her brother's double-wide trailer, at least 40 feet across, with raised dais and platforms with ceiling lights, directed to illuminate individual pieces. The place was dazzling and she couldn't quickly pick a favorite so quickly. The objects were all gold and red and sometimes green, speckles of color like a Georges Seurat.

"How can I possibly choose?"

"Please."

"I think... that one." Mia pointed to a tapestry on a far wall, in the corner, not the most prominent item. It was discolored and frayed on one side.

The woman from earlier entered and gave Mia iced water and handed a tea to Fong, then disappeared as quickly and quietly as she arrived.

"Interesting choice. Why that one, Doctor?"

"Please, just Mia is fine. Why do I like the tapestry? I don't know. I just went with my gut."

"But why do you think your gut selected that piece?"

"Because… it's damaged."

"Interesting."

"That tapestry looks like it must have been rescued. The fraying, the discoloration… It was exposed to moisture. I see some spots on it from mold. Although I'm certain you treated it to stop any more damage, it seems like someone put it in an attic and forgot about it. The condition it's in, I think that maybe… I think we're lucky. We're lucky it wasn't destroyed. That piece, I imagine, started out in a palace. After that, I can't say, but it wasn't treated well. And now here it is, back where it belongs. Inside a palace."

Mr. Hau smiled, but it was exactly the same smile. His mouth and eyes didn't budge. He nodded. "I like it, too."

"But you didn't restore it."

"You notice a lot, Mia." He sat down behind his desk, and she chose a chair opposite.

Mr. Hau continued his thought, "I need you to rescue something for me. Like that tapestry was rescued."

"Your assistant spoke to me over the phone, but I wasn't entirely clear on all of the details."

"A long way to travel when you don't know all the details."

"I suppose that's true."

"I read about you in the news. Quite the story."

"Of course. It's so embarrassing. It sometimes feels like that must've happened to someone else."

"I need you to find something for me." He opened up the drawer on his desk and produced a large envelope, the size of printer paper, and pushed it across the desk.

Mia opened it and removed a black and white

photograph. It was a profile picture of a young man, dressed almost like a soldier. He didn't have a gun or a helmet, though—instead, he wore a hat, almost like a baseball cap. He carried a dark box with both hands, no larger than a shoebox, with a design carved into it. Behind him were several other people. A young lady in pigtails, high school-aged, carried a rifle. Some grown adults in the background had their mouths open, maybe yelling. Mia could just make out a couple very meager homes in the background.

Mr. Hau clarified, "I would like that box."

"What is it?"

"I don't know."

"What's inside of it?"

"I don't know."

"Who's the young man in—"

Mr. Hau politely interrupted. "I know that I want this box and I know that you are the best person to find it for me, but I know that I want this box and I know that you are the best person to find it for me, but I'm afraid I don't have the answers to any of your questions, Mrs. Treadwell."

"With all due respect, Mr. Hau, how can you know that before I've asked them?"

"This photo came to me by chance. I barely paid attention to it at first, but when I looked closely, I fell in love with that box. I feel it belongs here, in this room, in this collection. I asked you which piece was your favorite and you went with your gut."

Mia nodded.

Mr. Hau continued, "It's like that for me, too. I saw this box and I felt a pull to it. You understand that feeling as well?"

"Yes. Of course."

"My gut feels a pull from that box. And like you with

that tapestry, after your gut told you what to do, you interrogated it, and learned why. I would like that box so I can do the same. I want to have it in front of me to understand why it calls to me. You strike me as a woman who would understand."

"I think so... and maybe I would do the same if I felt so drawn to something and I had the resources that you have, but..." She had a question, but she wasn't sure exactly what it was yet. She mentally bent the corner of that page in her mind, promising herself she'd return to it later. She asked her second biggest question: "Why me?"

"I read about your story, as I said."

"I understand that, but... I'm not an expert in Chinese history, let alone art history. I don't know the language. When I was on the phone with your assistant, I did my best to convince him that I wasn't the person for this job, but he was very insistent. I mean... there must be people more qualified to help you find this box, right?"

"No."

Mia waited for him to continue that thought, but the emptiness of it hung around for an awkward moment. Was she supposed to say something? She started to speak again and was quickly cut off before the first syllable.

"I've built this company from nothing. All of business is relationships, and all of it is built on need. The more needed you are, the taller your office is. I size people up quickly to do my job. I didn't want to give you all the details until you were here, in front of me, to see you in person. Now that I have, I know you're the right person."

"Well, I'm... I guess I'm honored you put so much faith in me."

"My assistant has already discussed the details of your remuneration. I hope the hotel is to your liking. Mr. Fong will take you wherever you need to go. He can arrange meetings with anyone you need to speak with and he can translate when necessary. You are in very good hands with him. Naturally, I will cover any incidental spending. Mr. Fong will keep me updated on your progress. Thank you for being my guest in Hong Kong. I look forward to seeing how you find me my box.""

Mr. Hau stood up and offered a hand. Mia stood up and shook it. She heard the door behind her open automatically and Fong stood by it, allowing Mia to exit. It seemed the meeting was over.

CHAPTER
FOUR

The driver took the Treadwells back down the elevator to the private parking garage and they all climbed in.

"Where to, ma'am?"

"I'm starving," said Raphael.

Mia nodded. "Me too, now that you mention it. Mr. Fong? Is there a place you could recommend?"

"What are you in the mood for?"

Raphael was quick to answer. "Nothing with the face still on it."

Mr. Fong smiled with half his mouth. "Do you like dumplings?"

"Sure," said Mia. Raphael nodded.

The driver took them westward out of the Central District, with its tall and modern structures and businesses. They followed the highway along the coast, and he took an exit into Sai Ying Pun.

It looked like a different city, less glass and more cement. The streets became narrower, the storefronts smaller. These twisty streets didn't share the glamor of the

Central District, just 15 minutes away. The place had character, though. Mostly built up before a regime of central planning, the place was a quilt of shapes and materials that hardly matched, with buildings where the top half didn't match the bottom in color or in shape. Buildings were often unpainted, or two-toned. It reminded Mia of when Raphael first became interested in LEGO and built charming nonsense.

The place was truly three-dimensional, with stairs and roads upward and downward, buildings built on hills with steep angles. Small windows were everywhere and most had neon signs or air-conditioners in them—a lot of things that would violate building codes back in New York. The signage came in all shapes and colors. The cars were smaller, and more appropriate for the confined area. Many Vespas, and most people traveled on their feet, no matter how old they were, carrying groceries and children and deliveries.

Fong parked outside of a small noodle shop, open on one side and facing the sidewalk like a food truck, with stools in a row by the bar. They got out.

"Is it okay to park here?" asked Mia.

"As I said at the airport, ma'am: no one will bother about this car."

They sat on the stools at the bar. Mr. Fong helped them find items on the menu they would like, and he ordered for them.

"How long have you been working for Mr. Hau?" Mia asked.

"Just about four years."

"He seems like an interesting guy."

"Yes, ma'am."

"Do you like it?"

"I do. Second best job I ever had."

"What was the best?"

He reached into his pocket and retrieved his cellphone, then flicked around a bit until he found what he was looking for. A video. He held it out so both of the Treadwells could see. They leaned in. He pressed play.

"I've seen this!" said Raphael.

The video was of a man beating up a half-dozen ski-masked assailants, performing extremely acrobatic, choreographed fights with very fake whooshes and pows when punches and kicks attacked and missed. After a few minutes of footage of the hero beating up bad guys in a warehouse, Fong paused the video.

Raphael said, "That's *Shaolin Assault Tiger IV*, right? Starring Donny Li."

Up close, Mia got a better look at his hands, where he held the phone. They were scarred, especially along the knuckles, with a distinct scar from stitches running along his left wrist. She asked, "You did stunts? For the movies?"

"I sure did."

"You don't look anything like Donny Li, though," said Raphael.

"I didn't do stunts for the actor. I did them for the guys in ski masks."

"Which one?" asked Raphael.

"All of them. It looks like there are a lot of attackers, but it's just me every time, and a few extras wearing the same outfit. A little movie magic."

"That's so cool," said Raphael, his mouth hanging open a little bit. "Didn't that hurt when he body slammed you into the table?"

"The floor in that spot had an inflatable cushion in it, but it was covered by a tarp, so it looked like concrete. They cut away just before you can see. The table was balsa wood."

"Seems like you are doing all the dangerous stuff."

"Donny Li does his own stunts, so don't sell him short. My job was to make him look as cool as possible. The more painful it looks for me, the more badass the star looks. Pardon my language, ma'am."

"Oh, he's heard much worse than that," said Mia.

The food arrived—soup and noodles for Mia and fried dumplings for the boys.

Raphael's hunger and curiosity with Mr. Fong came into direct conflict when he tried scarfing down his dumplings as quickly as possible while asking follow-up questions so that neither the eating nor questioning was working well. Mia encouraged him to choose one or at least to slow down.

"So you know Donny Li?"

"Yeah. We did a few movies together."

"Is he cool in real life?"

"He's a nice guy."

"Whoa. Where'd you learn to fight?"

"My dad and brothers a little. A gym where I grew up. I was at a Shaolin temple for about a year."

"No way!"

"It's not like you see in the movies. They're Buddhist monks, but there's barely any meditation or prayer. Mostly it's a lot of work and training to fight. All day, every day. They don't play around, either. They'll hurt you. They want to break people and weed them out. It's like *The 36th Chamber of Shaolin*, without the obstacle course."

"That's so badass!"

Mia nearly choked on her soup, coughed, and said, "Raphael!"

"What? You just said it was fine for me to hear!"

"Yes, but not to say."

Fong said, "There is a Shaolin Wushu Center not too far from here. It's not a real monastery, but the monks there do a lot of demonstrations and classes for tourists."

Raphael looked at his mother with hopeful eyes she'd seen a million times. Puppy dog eyes that said "please, please, please," without using any words.

"I don't know... I'm not sure I feel comfortable leaving you with strangers in a foreign country."

Fong said, "There's no place safer in the city, ma'am. I can vouch for that. Mr. Hau will pay for it. Think of it as an athletic summer day camp."

"Mom! It's physical education!"

"Okay, okay." Mia laughed.

"And it's like... cultural...enrichment."

"Raphael. You already talked me into it. You don't need to keep trying to make the sale."

The boys continued talking about Kung Fu movies for the rest of the meal. Mia tuned it out and started her research the way she always did: by checking her phone. But first, she looked up news about the woman on the plane.

A small local story was featured in *Oriental Daily News*, which Mia followed with a little help from translation software. Her name was Xiaoli Tao. The official cause of death was ruled as an accidental overdose of her prescription medications, though it didn't say what the prescription was. It said she was unmarried, had no kids, and that she worked as a "digital media consultant," but no employer was listed.

Mia thought about it for a moment. First, she focused on some details that didn't sit right with her. Xiaoli had no one to miss her after she was gone. Her legacy: died of accidental overdose. No family. Worked as a media consultant. As far as the history books knew, that was the sum of who she was. That didn't sit right with Mia, either.

THE WUSHU CENTER was just as her driver had described it. From the inside, it looked to her like a YMCA tai chi class. It was two stories, a square with an open courtyard garden in the middle, with no roof, just like many buildings Mia saw in Florence when she last saw her friend Aldo. Half the people there were tourists, mostly from England by the sound of the accents she heard. It looked as harmless as she could imagine. Mr. Fong didn't show a credit card, say his name, or anything else. He just told them to take care of Raphael for the day and just that was enough.

Mia tried hugging her son, but he was too embarrassed to let her in front of all the cool Kung Fu people. She gave him the usual warning that she always gave—don't wander off, and if something's wrong, call me immediately.

Mia and Mr. Fong got back in the car that was, once again, double-parked without any worry.

"What would you like to do now, ma'am?"

"I would like to... sit up front? Is that okay?"

"Yes, ma'am. That's fine."

She climbed out and got in the passenger seat and buckled up. "I do my best thinking when I'm driving. I can't drive here, but I am sitting on the left side of the car, so it kind of feels like I'm driving. I think this will work."

"Any special place you'd like to go?"

"Nope. Just as long as we're moving, that's good for me. If we were dancing, you'd be leading."

Mr. Fong smiled and nodded and put the car into drive.

Mia said, "I should start with what I know. Nothing. What don't I know?"

"Ma'am?"

"I'm sorry, I'm thinking out loud. I do that."

"Yes, ma'am."

"When was the photo taken? What were those clothes he was wearing? Where was the photo taken? Was he taking the box somewhere? Where did the box come from? Mr. Fong?"

"Yes, ma'am?"

"I couldn't help noticing that you have a lot of... what's the word I'm looking for... influence?"

"Not to be disagreeable, ma'am, but I don't have any pull. Who I represent does."

"Does that pull reach the university?"

"Yes, ma'am, it does."

CHAPTER
FIVE

HKU's campus was stunning. Mia walked through the thoroughfare with Mr. Fong and enjoyed the strange mixture of English colonial architecture, with its columns and open terraces, domed turrets, and immaculate rows of palm trees, all coexisting peacefully with the new structures. While the old buildings spoke with their details, the new spoke only with pure geometry: curves, bends, and glass, and hardly any color, like they were Silicon Valley products.

They consulted a visitor map and found their way to the department of art history. The humid air was getting hot and it was a relief to get inside an air-conditioned building. The students there were overwhelmingly women, judging by the people walking in the halls, and they walked past walls covered in samples of students' personal work.

They wandered into the faculty offices and no one stopped them. Mr. Fong poked his head into a room and asked the pretty young professor a question in Cantonese. She smiled, pushed some loose hair behind her ear, and answered. He kept walking and Mia followed until they found a door labeled Dr. Stephen Fadigan. Mia knocked on the door.

"Come in."

Mr. Fong opened the door and went in first. He pulled out a chair in front of the professor's desk and stood back against the wall with his arms crossed, and Mia could see his forearm muscles bulge.

"Doctor Fadigan?"

"Yes?" The balding man with a white beard and pink skin didn't leave his seat.

"Hi, professor. I'm Mia Treadwell. I was just hoping for a moment of your time."

"Mia Treadwell… your name sounds familiar." He spoke in a posh Southern English accent, the kind Mia always heard on the BBC.

"Well, we are colleagues, of a sort. I'm also an art historian. I was at NYU until just recently…"

He turned a bit and started typing into his computer. He looked at Mia, then back at whatever he just read about when he searched for her name. He leaned back in his chair. "Ah. Yes. Mrs. Treadwell. I know who you are." He spoke in exactly the same tone as he would to a derelict cousin who showed up at his home asking for money.

Mia sighed. Thanks to the internet, her reputation chased her to the other side of the Pacific. "I was just hoping you could look at a photograph. It's of a box, but I'm not an expert in—"

"I'm afraid I'm quite busy at the moment."

"Oh, this wouldn't take a minute—"

"Far too busy."

"Is there a time later when we could speak?"

"How long do you expect to be in Hong Kong, Mrs. Treadwell?"

"Oh, I don't know exactly, not more than a week, I imagine."

"I'll be busy for more than a week, I imagine."

"I see. Well. I'm sorry to bother you." She stood up and walked out the door, and once in the hall, she realized Mr. Fong hadn't followed her. She turned around to see her driver in the doorway. He held up a finger to show he'd be just a minute then closed the door, leaving her outside, alone in the hall.

She waited awkwardly, leaning on one foot after moving aside as a woman walked past. She folded her arms. The door opened again. Mr. Fong walked back to where he stood before. The professor's complexion was pinker than before, a little sweaty on the brow, and he worked on adjusting his necktie, which had suddenly become far too tight around his neck while Mia was out of the room. He drank deeply from a bottle of water.

"My schedule just cleared up, as it happens. What can I do for you, Dr. Treadwell?"

Mia took her seat again. She sat her backpack on her lap, opened it, and set the envelope on the desk. He took it and looked it over. Then he looked at Mia, awaiting further instructions.

"What can you tell me about that photo, Professor?"

"What's to say? This looks like a Red Guard carrying a box."

"I figured that much out on my own. What can you tell me about the box itself?"

The professor opened a drawer and fished around until he found a magnifying glass, then leaned in and got as close a look as he could. He spoke aloud his observations as he made them.

"Box looks... wooden. Red lacquer. On a very complex

relief. These carvings are very impressive. The clothing on the characters depicted on the box are distinctly Manchu. Qing Dynasty. I expect the artisan has had some influence from Bada Shanren. It's in the early Southern Chan Buddhist style. Individualist. But this might be a fake."

"A fake? Why do you say that?"

"The depth of the reliefs—and when I say depth, I mean the quality, not the depth of the carvings into the wood—is characteristic of very late Qing. That would be recent dynastic history, 1800s or so. As an expert in Christian Orthodox iconography, you'll be quick to understand that much of the art is simply political propaganda, to be quite blunt about it. It's like that in Europe and in China. Patronage was the name of the game. The people with the money are the people who decide what the art is."

Mia nodded. "I wouldn't use the word propaganda, but yes, I understand your meaning."

"Most people who commissioned art like this were lords, or they were people wealthy enough that they could buy it and gift it to a lord, to show fealty or as a bribe. The character of this rings of late Qing, but the characters depicted are not. They are Manchu lords, no doubt about that, but their clothing is relatively old fashioned by 100 years."

"So you date the style around the 1800s, but the fashion of the characters is in the 1700s?"

"Quite right."

"That's strange."

"You say it's strange, but it strikes me as unlikely. You see, these artists wouldn't necessarily even know what the wealthy elites' fashion looked like 100 years before they were born. And it's also unlikely they would carve something like this for a relatively unknown lord who was long gone. Obviously, it's better to make the characters in the art contemporary, so as to flatter the lords who are still alive." He chuckled to himself.

"Perhaps this was a deceased relative? Perhaps a wealthy person commissioned it to honor an ancestor."

"Possible. And sensible. However," he raised a finger to emphasize the point, "this is China. Skepticism is warranted."

"How so?"

"In the late 70s, after Mao Zedong died, the following administration was far more tolerant of old art. The market flooded with pieces that mysteriously re-emerged, and many were real. At first. But the value of these pieces was so extraordinary, a cottage industry of fakes flooded the market. You are surely aware of knockoffs? Copies of name-brand shoes and jeans and such? Well, you might say that these were knockoffs of artifacts. I wasn't here then, but the man who used to have this office was. He made quite a pretty penny, and retired early." He pointed at a spot on the photo. "You can see here, this?"

Mia leaned in. "Not really."

He handed her the magnifying glass so she could see.

"It's a bird," she observed.

"A red-crowned crane. Symbol of moral correctness, and virtue, especially for nobility. An endangered species now. This was owned by someone very important or it was made by a very talented artist who was a terrible forger."

Mia offered an alternative theory. "Is it possible the artist was simply ahead of their time?"

"Well, if that were the case, this box would be quite the find. The Southern style tried to capture brief glimpses of enlightenment through art, as the Buddhists would define it. If my cursory and, I might add, completely provisional analysis holds true, perhaps this artist was a Bodhisattva." He could see Mia wasn't familiar with the word. "That is to say, a person on the path to spiritual transcendence. A man ahead of his time, if you will."

Mia nodded along and her eyes drifted off far away as she organized her thoughts.

The professor added, "If it's genuine—and I would wager 10-to-1 that it's not—but if it's genuine, then it's a real shame." He looked up over Mia at Mr. Fong and swallowed hard. Mia twisted in her seat to see what the professor was looking at.

Mr. Fong said, "Don't worry, professor. I'm not a party member." The professor relaxed. Mia faced Dr. Fadigan and asked him to finish his thought.

"Why do you say it's a shame?"

"That box is certainly destroyed."

"How can you be so sure?"

"A Red Guard is holding it. This must have been taken in the 60s, when Chairman Mao inspired the youth of the mainland to rise up and continue his process of continuous, permanent revolution. These kids were like..." He snapped his fingers, trying to jog his memory. "The one with the American Amish devil children..."

Mr. Fong said, "*Children of the Corn*."

"Yes! They went on to destroy everything of the past. They wanted to start history from scratch, reset the calendar to Year Zero. They held Marx's ideas of the dialectic process, that there is an underlying paradise right in front of us, if only we weed out everything keeping it from us. That meant they needed to destroy the four Olds, as Mao called them: Old Ideas, Old Culture, Old Customs, Old Habits. This box was certainly destroyed, probably burned. And whoever had it before it was taken by those kids, they were almost certainly executed. Not only was this box old, it's Manchu."

"What's the significance of that?"

"Mrs. Trea—" He looked up at Mr. Fong quickly, then corrected himself. "Dr. Treadwell, I don't know how much you know of the history and culture of this part of the world. Ninety-percent of China is ethnically Han Chinese. The last 300 years of Chinese Dynastic history was the Qing: a Manchu Dynasty. A foreign occupation. There is still resentment over it to this day. The British Empire was very good at supporting kingdoms ruled by minority groups, because the minority could only stay in power with colonial help. This kept colonies loyal, you see. And the Qing capitulated, cowered, and ultimately disintegrated, much like the Roman Empire. Those bad feelings still linger, transgenerationally, as they often do."

"Your point is that they would have hated this box twice as much."

"That is precisely right. May I ask what your interest is in this box?"

"I'm looking on behalf of a, uh... interested party." She wasn't even sure she was saying it right.

"I see. Well. I'm sorry I couldn't give more optimistic news."

"No, that's alright. You've been very helpful. Oh, and one other thing. You said the box was red, but the photo is black and white. How can you know that?"

"That's a great question, actually. We have a lab here that does digital colorization of old black and white photographs. It's really impressive stuff. You can hardly tell they were originally black and white. And working in the same department as these people, I've learned a couple things, including how they know which colors to use where. A lot of it is just research. Some common sense. Some colors, however, are a matter of deduction."

He pointed at the star on the young man's cap. It clicked. Mia said, "The star is the same color of gray as the box. We know the star is red, so we can infer that the box must be also."

"Nicely done, Dr. Treadwell. Are you a *Star Trek* fan?"

She shook her head.

"You've certainly seen the costumes, yes? The colors on that show are just... garish. Very bright, primary colors. That show came out in the early 1960s when people were still transitioning between black and white to color TV. In color, you can see Captain Kirk wears a green shirt, but Lieutenant Uhura wears a red outfit. In black and white, you can't see the colors green and red, but you can distinguish the uniforms by the shades of gray."

"Thank you, Professor. You've been very helpful. I really do appreciate it."

She stood up and offered him a hand to shake. He reached out and stopped for a moment. Mia noticed that his middle finger was pink and purple and beginning to swell. He held out his other hand and awkwardly shook her right with his left.

"I accidentally slammed my finger in the car door this morning," he explained, his eyes darting to Fong, then back to Mia. He chuckled nervously.

CHAPTER
SIX

They found a café on campus and sat on the outdoor patio, despite the heat. Mia worked on her laptop, doing more research under the shade of the table's umbrella and taking the occasional sip of coffee. Finally, she closed her computer and looked directly at her driver.

"I'm sorry, but I need to talk about that."

"About what, ma'am?"

"Did you break that man's finger to force him to speak to me?"

"No, ma'am."

"I find that hard to believe."

"I tightened his tie because he was rude to you. He called you missus. He is your colleague. He should have said doctor. The finger was an accident."

"That's right, though, I did say that to you at the airport, didn't I... But hurting him and strangling him with his tie wasn't necessary."

"I'm sorry."

"You should be apologizing to him, not me."

"I'm only sorry to you, ma'am. I won't apologize to that man."

Mia grumbled, putting her face in her hands. She sighed and leaned on her elbows. "I know I'm a foreigner and I don't know how things work around here, but I would appreciate it if you would not break anyone else's anything for the rest of my trip."

"I won't make promises I can't promise I'll keep, ma'am."

"You seem like such a nice guy. I'm disappointed in you, Mr. Fong." Mia realized she had accidentally slipped into Mom Voice. Mr. Fong seemed immune to it. He looked around the courtyard, pretending he saw something interesting. Mia sighed again and said, "It's okay. You can ask."

She had his attention again. "Ask what, ma'am?"

"Why the professor was rude to me."

"It's none of my business."

She waved toward herself as if coaxing some invisible smoke.

He said, "I am a little curious."

"Come on, tough guy."

"Ma'am, why was that man you just met so rude to you?"

Mia took a sip of her coffee. "I'll tell you some other time."

"What? You can't—" He caught himself forgetting his professionalism and regained his composure.

Mia laughed and said, "You know I was teaching at NYU, right?"

Fong nodded.

"I, uh... I wrote a paper. A controversial paper. It got some bad attention. And one of my students..." She paused. She'd told the story so many times and she still hated to.

"As I said, ma'am, it's not my business."

Mia returned to working on her computer again. She uploaded a digital copy of the photo and did a reverse image search. She checked sales records. She spent an hour looking in all the obvious places before stopping herself.

"This is stupid. Hau's people must have already looked in all the obvious places. Mr. Fong?" He perked up. "Do you know if your boss hired anyone else to look into this?"

"You mean, another private investigator? Yes, a local agency."

"Oh, ha, no, I'm not..." She had a brief realization. "Wait. Am I a private investigator?"

"Well, ma'am, you're investigating. And you don't work for the police. You told that professor that you work on behalf of an interested party."

"Oh, wow. I did say that. I guess I am."

She pushed away from the distraction of her own career title, suddenly concerned that she might need a license to do her new job. She thought out loud, "Something's not right. They must have found something, right? Why didn't Mr. Hau share what they found with me?"

"That's not for me to say, ma'am."

"No, I'm sorry. I wasn't really asking, I'm just talking to myself. Unless... was it the investigators who found this photo?"

Fong didn't say anything but his silence gave her the answer. She continued asking herself questions. "He must know that if a Red Guard had the box, it would probably be destroyed. So why is he so certain it wasn't burned?" She thought about that tin of candies.

Mia searched online for any chemical labs that conduct

testing for the public. Instead, she found something called AliveToDance—a non-profit that would test people's party drugs for free and send back reports about what was in them, part of a philosophy of harm reduction. Mostly it looked like they tested drugs such as molly for fentanyl or other dangerous additives. Mia looked for a lab. In the contact section, it implied that testing would be expedited for donations. The nearest lab was in Darwin, Australia.

"I need a carrier that does overnight airmail."

Fong nodded and stood up.

She checked the time and it was already almost 6 p.m. "Oh, wow, I totally lost track of time! We have to go pick up Raphael."

The rain started pouring without warning and the windshield wipers could barely keep up.

Fong was about to step out when Mia interrupted, "No need for both of us to get soaked. I'll be quick."

She got out and ran inside the post office. The area was smaller than the waiting room of most oil change places she'd been to. She asked the man behind the counter if he spoke English, and he nodded. She asked for an envelope and to get it shipped as quickly as possible.

She opened up her backpack, found Xiaoli's tin, placed one of her candies into the bag, and wrote a quick note. She sealed it, wrote the address in Darwin on the front, and handed it to the man. He rang her up. When he told her the price, she was shocked. Then she remembered to do the conversion to US dollars. The price was still shocking.

She pointed to the car outside and asked, "Do you know that car?"

He shrugged.

"That's the car I came in. That's Hau Junjie's car."

The man nodded and completed the sale without payment.

"Hey, can I ask you something? Do you get paid by Mr. Hau, or..."

"Yes, of course."

"Okay. I was just checking."

WHEN THE CAR pulled up in front of the school, Raphael ran out and climbed inside.

"How was it? Did you have fun?"

Raphael just shrugged. Mia asked a few follow-up questions, hoping to prime the pump, but he wasn't interested in talking.

"Mr. Fong noticed that your mom is a private investigator. So that's pretty cool, right?"

"Yeah." He kept his face in his phone.

"What exactly is your job description, Mr. Fong?"

"I'm a chauffeur."

"I feel like you do so much more than that, though."

"Yes, ma'am, that's true."

They drove slowly. The water in the streets were a half-inch thick, the heavy, tropical rain coming down so fast the gutters couldn't drain it fast enough.

FONG DROPPED off the Treadwells at the hotel, under the awning so they wouldn't get wetter. He waited until he could see they were inside, then drove out. He swung by a small grocery store and picked up a few things. While he was inside, the rain let up, gone as quickly as it arrived.

Next, he drove to Sham Shui Po District, a part of the city he wouldn't take Mia and Raphael to. A place where the awnings in front of stores were made with particleboard and corrugated steel sheets, recovered from a demolished building across the street. Where the white, lead-based paint chipped and peeled, and fell like petals into the rainbow-black puddles of rain and motor oil.

Fong parked his car at the curb and no one disturbed it. Carrying a plastic bag, he stepped into an alley, into the T-shaped intersection between three buildings. The window air conditioners hummed loudly, like a swarm of machine insects, and they spit out hot air like car exhaust. No street lamps lit up this alley, and Fong was careful not to step on the debris in it: a bundle of fence wire, half a bike, an air conditioner that had fallen out of one of these windows.

He saw a black cat perched on top of a tire. Looking up, he spotted a man leaning out his window, eyeing another cat that was licking its hind paw, all of six floors down. He finished a beer and dangled the green bottle out the window, aiming for the cat. His hand released it. The bottle fell. It gained speed and power. The cat didn't see it coming. It landed and shattered next to the animal, and the cat jumped five feet and fled into the hiding places it knew well. The man laughed and vanished back into his apartment.

He found a door and two young men blocking the elevator asked him what he wanted. He pushed past them and took the elevator up to the eleventh floor. The elevator smelled like wet carpet and it made a rattling sound that didn't inspire confidence. It opened and Fong stepped out. He could smell someone cooking in one apartment. He could also smell that someone needed to take out their trash in another. He took the keys out of his pocket and went into 1104.

He spoke in Cantonese as he entered the home. "Grandma?"

The place was an oasis in this neighborhood. Perfectly clean and tidy. It wasn't much, but it was hers, and she made sure to keep it up to her standards. He walked through the living room, which was furnished exactly the same as when Fong was a toddler. He found her in the kitchen, watching something on a tiny television on the tiny kitchen table. She was eating fried pork intestines.

"Hello, Michael." She smiled.

He sat across from her. "This neighborhood is getting worse all the time."

"It's fine."

"It's not fine. Why not come stay with me? I have a good job. I make good money. I have a nice place."

"I'm happy for you, but I live here. Thank you for the groceries. You're a good boy."

"Trying to be."

"You are. And find a wife soon. Worry about that first. When you have a wife, then maybe. Have you been taking the yu jin I gave you?"

"I don't have menstrual cramps."

"It isn't just for that!" She smacked him on the head. "It's good for any kind of pain. You've been putting it on your knee, like I said?"

"Yeah, I tried it. It's okay but..."

"It helps circulation. You must not be using enough. You're probably suffering from a qi stagnation because you don't eat enough. I'll make you something."

"Thanks."

CHAPTER SEVEN

In the morning, Mia gathered her things from the mess she made on the hotel desk.

Raphael came out of the bathroom as she packed her backpack. Before they left, she tried eating a croissant as quickly as she could, courtesy of breakfast room service on Mr. Hau's tab.

"You excited to get back to the Kung Fu school?"

He shrugged.

She stopped chewing. "What's wrong?"

"Nothing."

"You don't want to go back?"

He shrugged again.

"Raphael. If you were excited to go back, you'd just say so. When you shrug, I know you aren't. So why not?"

"It's just not what I expected." He sat down on the chair at the desk.

"Why not?"

"It's not a real school. Not for me, anyway. They just put me in with all the tourists doing kata and boring stuff like that. The real school is for locals."

"So just tell them you want to do the real school."

He shrugged again. "Also, it's Wushu, not Kung Fu." He looked at his mom's mess on the desk. He picked up the picture and looked at it for a moment and said, "Nice."

"What do you mean, nice?"

"That truck in the photo. That's a GAZ-69. It's like a Russian Jeep."

"You know, most boys your age would get excited about a Corvette, not some Soviet jalopy. I guess it technically counts as a classic car. Are these army green?"

"Yeah, usually."

"I like army green. It's a very... earthy color."

Raphael rolled his eyes and headed for the door.

WHEN THEY WENT DOWNSTAIRS to the lobby, Fong was already there, sitting comfortably in a chair and enjoying a coffee. He stood up as soon as he saw them. "Good morning, ma'am. Raphael."

"Good morning, Michael. Listen, um, it seems that Raphael was not enjoying himself at the school, so I think we need to give him something else to do or else he'll be coming with us all day."

"Why didn't you like it?"

"They put me with the tourists. I didn't get to do any of the cool stuff."

"The real school is for real students. You look like a tourist to them. You have to show them that you are really interested."

"I told them, though. I know they understood me in English, but they acted like they didn't."

"They aren't playing around in there, and they don't

want to waste a second on people who aren't serious. You don't tell them. You have to show them."

"How? How did you get in?"

"I had experience already, and I'm local and speak the language. That helps. Those instructors usually refuse to speak to students in another language, even if they can speak it. What I did was just join the class."

"How do you just join?"

"I showed up and didn't let them kick me out. You think you can do that?"

"I think so."

"It sounds easy, but it isn't. They'll try to bully you. They'll make you want to leave. You just have to show them you're serious."

Mia interrupted, "I don't know, Michael, that sounds maybe too rough."

Raphael scowled. "No. I can do that."

"Are you sure?" Mia asked.

He nodded.

"Well, if you have any problem, promise you'll call me? We'll come and get you right away."

Raphael said, "No. If I call my mom they'll know I'm not serious."

Fong smiled at him and that gave Raphael all the confidence he needed.

As they watched Raphael walk in through the double doors of the school, Fong said, "He'll be fine."

Mia forced a smile and nodded.

"Where to next, ma'am?"

She thought for a moment. She got out her phone and

took a photo of the black and white picture, then put both away.

"How about I just start driving. It'll help you think."

"Thank you. That's a great idea."

Fong put the car into drive. Mia looked out at the clutter of signs that seemed to cover every wall. "Why did you stop making movies? Is that an okay thing for me to ask?"

He cleared his throat. "Yes, ma'am. It started to take its toll. Injuries start to add up. They're quite good about safety in films these days, but accidents happen."

"Sounds a lot like an athlete."

"Yes, ma'am, I'd say that's a fair comparison. It was already getting to be too much when I met Mr. Hau. He offered me a job at just the right time. I owe him a lot."

Mia took the photo in her hand and looked at it, covering every inch, looking for any detail. Raphael had mentioned the truck. She looked at it. To Mia, it looked like every other truck. It seemed funny to her that his eyes went straight for the truck, but Mia barely noticed it. Maybe the rules of composition, drawing the eye to areas of the image, worked differently for different people.

At a red light, Mia asked, "When you look at this picture, where do your eyes go first?" She held the picture up.

He looked over. "I suppose... the girl in the back. With the pigtails."

"Interesting." She looked at the picture again, then held it up so he could see. "Why?"

"She looks possessed to me, ma'am."

Mia looked again. Now that he said it, she did look possessed.

"What is this on the car? Something wrapped around the window frame. Looks a little like... tinsel."

The light went green. Fong started driving again. "I'm certain it isn't Christmas decorations, ma'am."

"Is it some... Chinese tradition? Decorating a car like that?"

"Not where I'm from, ma'am. China is a big country, so I couldn't say it isn't a tradition somewhere else."

Street vendors selling knockoffs of Western products. Electronics shops selling Huawei phones and phone cards. Noodle shops. A grocer. A florist. It seemed like this was a place where small businesses still existed. Mia felt like she hardly saw those anymore.

When they came to a stop at a red light, Mia looked at it and spaced out a moment. Then, she looked at the picture. She looked at the gray star that she knew was red. She looked at the box. She looked at the truck that she knew was green. She looked at the "tinsel" on the truck.

"Hold on. Stop here."

Fong double-parked. Mia got right out and walked up to the florist, saying hello to the woman arranging yellow chrysanthemums. The woman shrugged and answered in Chinese. Mr. Fong quickly joined Mia to translate.

"Could you tell me what this plant is? On this truck?"

Fong repeated what she said to the woman, who was uncooperative and too busy to talk about Mia's problems. Fong pointed to the car. Mia didn't understand what he said except the name Hau Junjie came up. The woman finally answered, and Fong told Mia. "She says it's sueda."

"What is sueda?"

Fong relayed the question and answer. "It's a... I don't know the English word exactly. It's like a seaweed. A sea-blite?" The florist nodded.

Mia asked her, "Is it red?" She pointed at the plant that was the same gray tone as the star on the young man's cap.

She nodded and added some things. Fong translated, "It's green in the spring and summer, but it becomes bright red in autumn. It's a marsh plant. She says if you want to see it, go to Red Beach."

"Thank you so much, ma'am."

They got back into the car. Mia opened her laptop and connected to the internet through a hotspot. She started typing it out, just as Fong explained.

"Red Beach is in Panjin. It's far north on the mainland."

Mia found images. A marsh of impossibly brilliant bright red. The photos were incredible. The red went on to the horizon. She read further, speaking one portion out loud. "It's a natural preserve, home to several endangered species, including the red-crowned crane. That's the bird on the box. Mr. Fong, I think I have a good idea about where the photo was taken."

"Yes, ma'am. May I just say, you are very good at this."

"You may, Mr. Fong." She leaned back into her seat with a proud little smile. "I think we earned ourselves a treat."

"You want to go to a bar, ma'am?"

She laughed. "No, I was thinking more like ice cream."

"That sounds excellent, ma'am."

CHAPTER
EIGHT

They were three blocks away from the ice cream shop that Fong had recommended when they stopped at a red light. Two motorbikes turned onto their street, stopping directly in front of the car. The bikes were in poor condition, one rigged for offroading, the other a rusty motor scooter. The men riding them weren't wearing helmets or leather. One was in a white undershirt and a baseball cap, the other wore a windbreaker, had balding hair and bad teeth, and was smoking a cigarette.

The light turned green. Fong honked at them a couple times, and the two men said something to each other in Chinese, pointing at the car. Finally, Fong cut the wheel to try to get around them. When he was halfway across the median, the man in the undershirt scooted ahead a few feet to keep him blocked in.

Fong said, "Stay in the car." He got out and pointed at the men as he approached them.

Mia didn't know the specifics of what Fong said to them, but based on the tone and body language, and the reactions of the bikers, it was full of profanity and threats.

They yelled back at him, waving their hands and pointing. Cars behind them were honking to get Fong to move.

Hearing the rumble of three more bikes, Mia looked out the back window. The bikers were as shabbily dressed as the one Fong was arguing with: one in a tracksuit, one in cargo pants and a Hawaiian shirt with a neck tattoo of a woman, and one in jeans and no shirt at all. The men's bikes were just as shabby as their hygiene.

Mia leaned across the console and honked the horn. Fong looked around to see the others, winding around the honking, frustrated cars behind the Rolls. They parked their bikes just behind the car, blocking them in on two sides. The three men got off their bikes and retrieved various makeshift weapons they brought with them: a large chef's knife, an aluminum baseball bat, and an ordinary hammer. Quickly, Mia rolled up the windows and locked the door.

Fong saw them and whipped around to face the two men he'd just been yelling at. The man in the windbreaker reached behind him for something. Fong was quicker in real life than he was in his movies. He pulled something from the pocket of his black pants, and with the smooth motion of his arm, his whole body following it, a telescoping baton extended almost two feet long and struck the biker in the face.

He hit the pavement and dropped a homemade pistol zip gun built out of aluminum and scrap wood. The man in the undershirt grabbed at him, getting his sports jacket. Fong effortlessly slipped out of it, backed away, and struck the man, who blocked with his arm. The baton caught his wrist, which he grabbed with his free hand. He shouted in pain and leaned down.

Mia's hands went right to her face and she shouted something unintelligible, like, "Ohmygoshnostop!" After struggling to get her phone, she dialed 911 but got an error message. Two of the reinforcements ran right past the car and Mia, joining the fight against Fong. The one with the aluminum bat tried to open her door.

Fong was waving wildly, stepping backward, to keep the three men from getting close to him.

When the man with the bat couldn't get in easily, he wound back and took a swing. Mia bent over the console, expecting a shower of glass. The bat made a loud *bonk* sound and Mia looked up to see only a small dent. Armored windows. He took a few more swings, chipping small pieces. He jumped onto the trunk of the car, over onto the roof, and began cracking the bat against the windshield with every muscle he could rally, like splitting logs with an ax.

Mia tried calling 911 again. It still didn't work.

Fong was keeping the others at bay, but every step away from them was a step away from Mia. He was already right in the middle of the four-way stop. People were honking their horns and shouting out their windows. Others pulled out cell phones and started recording.

The small chips on the windows of the car were multiplying and beginning to connect with jagged lines. The window was strong but not invulnerable. Moving over to the driver's side, Mia tried to familiarize herself with the controls. With everything on the opposite side, she felt like she was on her first day of driver's ed. She put the car into drive and slammed on the acceleration.

The machine had a lot of hustle and it sped out faster than she expected. She forgot that Fong had turned the wheel all the way to the right. The car raced across the street, over the curb, and slipped into an alley. An earsplitting screech sounded as the sides scraped the alley, which was just barely too narrow. Both side mirrors came right off and the car squeezed between two buildings, then stopped.

She gunned the engine again but was stuck. Smoke was coming from the other side of the hood. She realized she had pushed the scooter into the alley with her and mangled it into a steel and plastic wad, now pinned under the front.

Putting it in reverse, Mia looked behind in the rearview mirror. The man who was on the roof a moment ago was in the street, recovering from his fall and looking for his baseball bat. She slammed on the accelerator, but the car still wouldn't budge. That damn bike under the car, and the doors didn't have an inch of room to open on either side. She fiddled with the console, pressing every button she could find. The hazards turned on, the windshield wipers began, and a car emergency service called a recording of a voice that began asking questions about the nature of the emergency in Chinese.

Finally, she found the button to the sunroof. It opened, slowly. She looked back in the rearview. The man had found his bat and was looking around, gathering his senses. She looked back at the roof. It was opened a third of the way, and some sunlight poured in. She felt the weight of the car shift and, in the rearview mirror, she saw his boots standing on the truck. The roof was two-thirds open now, and she pressed the reverse button to close it again. Looking up, she saw he was back on the roof, staring down at her with a grimace on his face and a little blood in his teeth.

She tried to shrink down as small as she could. He couldn't swing the bat at her, so he prodded at her with the tip. She blocked herself with her hands and forearms, which meant she had to release the button. The sunroof was still half open and Mia was too busy defending herself from the attacks to do anything else.

Then, a blur. The man rolled off the roof, over the windshield, and into the alley. A man stood up, but it wasn't the other guy. It was Fong.

He'd tackled the man. His eye and nose were bloody and his shirt was torn. He jumped back onto the hood and reached into the sunroof. Mia took his hand and he helped her out. No sooner than she was on the roof with him than she saw the other four men in the alley entrance behind them, every bit as beat up as Fong, and angry as hell. Mia reached into the car and grabbed her backpack. They hopped off the car, over the baseball bat guy, and ran deeper into the alley. The men behind them hurdled the car easily.

A man in the alley was smoking a cigarette and holding a door open with his body so it wouldn't lock behind him. "Hold that door!" yelled Mia. The man lazily smoked his cigarette, not reacting at all, until he saw the trouble that followed Mia and Fong. His eyes got big, he flicked his cigarette away and slipped back inside. The pair weren't ten feet away from an escape, watching the door closing in front of them.

Mia whipped her bag at the door. It landed just on the threshold. With two inches to spare, it stopped the door from closing. Fong let Mia in first, and he grabbed her bag on his way in. The door started closing on its own, slowly from the commercial door closer.

A factory. A cacophony of sewing machine noises. Row after row of men and women, mostly foreigners in Hong Kong to work, completely focused on their tasks. Almost 60 people. As the door was just about to close, four fingers slipped in.

Fong kicked the door and the man on the other side yelled out. Fong braced himself against the door. So did Mia. They both pushed back against the men outside, tilting forward 45 degrees, putting all their legs and back into it. Fong saw the man who was smoking and yelled something at him. He stood there, not 10 feet away, hands in his pockets, and shook his head. Fong yelled again.

The Nigerian seamstress closest to them finally saw what was happening, deafened to it from the clatter of the machines, and looked up as if just coming out of a sewing trance. She said something in broken Chinese.

The smoking man told her, "Mind your business. Get back to work."

She stood up, confronted her boss, and plucked the cigarette out of his mouth. He stammered a confused condemnation of her behavior. She walked up and handed the cigarette to Mia.

"I'm not in the mood for a cigarette right now!"

Fong took the cigarette from her and put it out on the crushed, purple fingers that jammed in the door. After a hiss and sizzle, the fingers slipped out and the door shut. There was a lot of cursing outside through the door, which they could hear even with all the noise.

Feeling every muscle in their bodies relax, they both collapsed against the door. They could feel the helpless bangs against the door trying to open it again.

The floor manager said, "I don't want any trouble." He put up his hands as though he were being robbed.

Fong stood up and thanked the woman. He gave the manager his cigarette back, extinguished, bent, and a little bloody. Mia stood up, too. The place had no ventilation and was ferociously hot. Fong led Mia past all the workers, into the next room where a second group was boxing up knockoff shoes that bore the logos of Reebok and Nike.

"We can't go out front. They'll be waiting for us there." Fong found an elevator, but it had an out-of-service sign on it. They went into the stairwell and began their ascent. Mia looked up the gap and the squared spiral that scaled up at least ten floors. They went up and up.

"I tried calling 911."

"It's 999 in Hong Kong."

"I should have known that. That was stupid of me."

"Smart people don't know everything, ma'am."

"Who are those guys?" Mia asked, her voice echoing in the vertical, concrete tunnel.

"Triads."

"That's like the mafia, right?"

"Kind of."

"Why did they attack us?"

"Probably saw the nice car and wanted to rob us."

Mia put a hand on his arm and stopped him. "C'mon. People around here know exactly who owns that car. People will let you double-park anywhere and give you anything you want on a tab. Those guys must know who you work for."

"Sometimes people hire them as muscle."

"What kind of people?"

"People who don't want anyone to know who they are. People who can pay?" He started walking again.

Mia followed him but didn't stop her questions. "Who, though?"

"I don't know."

They reached the top floor and opened the roof access. Instead of stepping out onto an empty, featureless roof, like the kind Mia had been on in New York, this roof was populated with two dozen people of all ages. A tent city, just like under bridges and on sidewalks in Denver. A portable radio somewhere was playing rap music. A man was cooking tripe on a small grill. They walked through this small, homeless village.

Fong walked to the edge and looked over the side. "They're still down there, covering the exits." He walked to another edge where there was a makeshift bridge built from three ladders and plywood. He started to cross it.

Mia looked down into the alley below. "No thank you."

"Come on. It's safe."

"There's no way you can know that it's safe."

"No dead people in the alley, are there?"

"That's not reassuring."

Fong reached out a hand to help her across. She took a baby step, letting herself feel the balance. "Nope. No way." She got down and crawled across it on all fours, where the center of gravity was as low as possible and she didn't have to rely on balance and light winds. She stood up when she got to the other side.

Another rooftop, just the same as the last. Here, camping tents were held together with duct tape. A woman was hanging up wet laundry on a line. An electrical line and an extension cord running across the ground, stealing from another building, powered several appliances used by five people running off the same power strip. Homes were made out of recovered corrugated metal and plastic sheets. One particularly interesting teepee was constructed from metal pipes and a car cover.

They crossed another alley with a much safer-looking bridge into what was something like a market, with people selling everything from sports tickets to wristwatches. Fong looked into the street, 10 flights down. Mia looked, too. The men were still around them, all had their faces on their phones, occasionally looking around.

"How are they still following us?"

There was a rumble as an elevated passenger train passed right over them on a track that wound its way between the buildings like an iron snake. Mia looked behind. She saw the man in the tracksuit and the man without a shirt.

"They're here!" She ducked down behind a makeshift, open-air appliance area, which had an unbalanced washing machine banging wildly as it ran, a loud humming refrigerator, and a microwave sitting on a wooden coffee table.

Fong went the other direction and dissolved into the crowd. Mia peeked. The men were checking their phones again, and one pointed in her direction. She looked at the microwave next to her. Pulling the phone out of her pocket, she put it inside the microwave and shut the door. She peeked again. The two men looked frustrated, complaining to each other. They looked around and cussed. No-shirt made a phone call, said some words, then hissed through his teeth. He ended the call and patted his accomplice on the chest with the back of his hand. The two walked off the way they came.

Fong came back to Mia.

"Where did you go?"

"I saw this and thought it might be useful." He showed her the long metal pipe he had found. "I guess they gave up looking."

"No. They lost the signal."

"What do you mean?"

Mia pointed at the microwave. "I thought it was strange

they were able to follow us so precisely. So I put my phone in the microwave."

"You cooked your phone?"

"No, but microwaves block radio waves, apparently. As soon as I put my phone in, they got frustrated and left. They kept checking their phones, did you notice that?"

"Yeah."

"They were tracking us through my phone."

A homeless woman approached with a bowl of soup and reached for the door of the microwave. Mia intercepted and stood between her and the cooking appliance.

"No no no no no!" she said urgently. "Please don't open that."

"I'm not eating this cold. Get out of my way," she said.

"Um, can I buy it? The microwave, not the soup." Mia went into her bag for her wallet, pulled out a generous amount of cash, and handed it to the woman. She was happy to take it and left.

Fong unplugged the microwave and picked it up. "I guess it's safe to go down now."

They headed back down the stairs.

"In New York," Mia explained, "the homeless live underground. They hide in the subway tunnels, under bridges. I've never seen anything like that. It's just... terrible."

"Yes, ma'am. Housing prices have gotten out of control. COVID-19 made it worse. The worst are in my grandmother's neighborhood. She could have ended up on a roof like this."

When they got back to the street level, they kept their eyes peeled for the gangsters as they headed back to where the attack started. The street was swarming with Hong Kong police in navy pants and light blue shirts, taking photos, interviewing witnesses, and trying to clear the street. One man with a pickup truck was having the challenge of his career trying to figure out how to get the car unwedged from the alley.

A witness saw Mia and Fong, pointed at them, and got the police's attention. A few immediately flocked over, knocking the microwave down onto the ground and arresting them. They didn't resist but the police were rough, anyway.

CHAPTER NINE

Mia paced back and forth inside the small room of white-painted bricks, feeling like a fish inside a tank. There was a table and a pair of chairs she could sit on, but she couldn't stay still. She looked up occasionally at the black sphere in the corner of the ceiling that housed a surveillance camera. There was no clock in the room and no windows to the outside, and no way to know how long she'd been inside.

Finally, a door opened and a woman in plainclothes came in, with a small laptop under her arm.

"Please, I have to call my son—"

"My name is Detective Cheung. Please have a seat."

"You don't understand—"

"Please have a seat and you can explain it to me."

Mia sat in one of the hard-plastic and metal stackable chairs. Her leg didn't agree with the decision, and it bounced restlessly.

Detective Cheung sat across from her, set her computer on the desk, and opened it. "Now then, please continue what you were saying."

"My son is at the Shaolin Kung Fu Center. I mean, Wushu. I get that mixed up. He was expecting me to come pick him up a half-hour ago. We've been in here for hours, I think, and no one would speak to us."

The detective typed quickly, nodding, and said, "We can have an officer swing by and pick him up."

"Oh, thank you. Please. We're not from here. I'm sure he's been calling me."

The detective reached into her pocket and produced a phone and gave it to Mia.

"Thank you. Thank you." She took the phone and dialed. It rang and rang. She hung up and sent a text saying, *This is mom. Please pick up.* She dialed again and this time, he picked up.

"Mom?"

"Hi, Raphael! Is everything okay?"

"Yeah! I did what Mr. Fong said and—"

"I'm glad, honey. Listen, I'm running late. So just hang tight a little longer and me or a police officer will come by and check in on you, okay? If you have any trouble, just call this number, okay?"

"Okay? What's going on?"

"Long story. I'll tell you when I see you, okay?"

"Okay."

"Love you. I'll see you soon."

"'Kay."

She hung up and handed the phone back to the detective. "Thank you."

"Not a problem. I have two myself so I understand. Now, Dr. Treadwell, I'd like to ask you some questions about what happened today."

The detective asked the basic questions that Mia expected and she gave honest answers. The detective wrote down extensive notes. She asked when Mia came into the city, what her business was, where she'd been the last few days, where she was staying, and her room number. She asked about the fight. She asked many questions about Mr. Fong and Mr. Hau, but Mia didn't have much to say about them.

"I didn't say anything about Mr. Hau."

"Yes, but Mr. Fong works for him and the car is in his name."

"Oh, right. Of course." Mia explained what she was doing in the country.

"And where is the box?" asked the detective.

"Well, I don't know yet. I've only been here three days."

"Do you have any promising leads?"

"Well... maybe. I don't know."

"Who else have you spoken to about this job?"

"Oh, uh... Mr. Fong, of course, um... a professor at HKU..." Mia stopped herself. She cleared her throat. "Hey, I'm just asking, because I don't know the laws. Do I have the right to an attorney?"

"Not during the investigative phase. If charges are pressed, then yes, you would. So, not at this time. Do you have a reason to need an attorney?"

"No, I just don't know my rights."

"If you cooperate and did nothing wrong, then you won't need your rights."

Mia shifted in her seat. "And I don't have the right to silence, either, I presume."

"That is correct. But silence is only an asset for the guilty, so I see no reason for you to need it."

Mia didn't answer. The room was quiet, and she wondered if she was doing something that would implicate her guilt, so she filled the emptiness by saying

"I guess"—a statement that she silently scolded herself for.

"Now, what was the name of the professor you spoke to?"

"Oh, uh... I don't remember." Mia was bad at lying.

"What department does he work in?"

Fadigan wasn't a pleasant man, but Mia didn't want to get him in trouble either. Or Fong, for that matter, if Fadigan mentioned his broken finger. Her heart and mind were racing. She couldn't think of a single thing she could say to put the detective off track.

A knock on the door felt like the bell ringing in a boxing match. A man came halfway in without being invited and said something in Chinese to the detective. She said something back, clearly annoyed by the interruption.

Then, to Mia, she said, "Just a moment, please." She stood up and stepped out of the room. Mia was alone again. The laptop was sitting there, open. She wanted to reach for it and see what she was typing. Mia looked up at the camera. Then at the computer. She sat perfectly still.

The door opened again. Detective Cheung stepped halfway in and said, "Dr. Treadwell, you are free to go."

MIA WAS PROCESSED before they released her. They passed her belongings back to her, including the microwave with her phone inside, and buzzed her through a thick metal door into a waiting area at the front of the police station. Mr. Fong was already there, a cut on his nose and lip and a big, purple bruise on his cheek. He smiled, walked up, and took the microwave from her.

"Thanks. That was getting heavy."

When they stepped outside, it was already getting dark. The streetlights were on and the signage was glowing. It must have rained because the streets were wet, casting distorted reflections of the neon light. A car was waiting for them, identical to the one Mia had destroyed, except this one was yellow. It was double-parked and idling. A man dressed in a suit stepped out, popped the trunk, and nodded. Fong put the microwave into the trunk and got into the driver's seat. Mia climbed into the passenger seat.

"What about him?" asked Mia.

"He'll take a cab. Shall we get Raphael now, ma'am?"

"Yes, please!"

Mr. Fong started driving. "We changed colors to avoid being noticed again."

"I didn't think they would let us go. That detective didn't seem very friendly."

"Mr. Hau has a lot of pull in this city, ma'am. He made a call."

She imagined the smashed luxury car. "How am I going to explain crashing his car? I can't pay for that!"

"Don't worry about that, ma'am. It wasn't your fault and Mr. Hau understands that."

A slight trickle started and Fong turned on the windshield wipers.

"The detective asked a lot about you and Mr. Hau."

"Did she." He said it like it wasn't a question. "What did she ask?"

"I don't know. Normal things, like about the job. She left her computer out when she stepped out of the room. I'm kicking myself for not looking."

"You did the right thing. That's a police trick. If you had looked, they would have seen that as a sign of guilt. You were right not to check. Ma'am, I'd like to say something, but I'm afraid it wouldn't be appropriate..."

"No, please, Michael. What is it?"

"You are a very smart woman, but Hong Kong is not a city where you can afford to be so naïve." He remembered a half-second later to add, "Ma'am," as if to soften the impunity of his unprofessional remark.

Mia sighed and nodded. "Maybe I'm not cut out for this kind of thing. I only wanted to look for a piece of art. I'm not a hard-boiled detective. I don't know anything about this gangster stuff, about cell phone tracking. And I brought Raphael here! It's too much! There's more going on here. You're right, I can be naïve sometimes. I think better of people than they deserve. But I'm not so naïve that I don't get that this is bigger than it looks. Michael, what is so special about this box?"

"I spoke with Mr. Hau an hour ago. He's very happy with our progress. He anticipated that you might feel concerned about security for you and your son, so he's already agreed to add security for you at the hotel. He's also publicly offered a reward to anyone who can identify those gangsters. And Mr. Hau has offered to increase your pay."

"They didn't get caught?"

"No, ma'am."

"That's all very generous of Mr. Hau, but I'd feel much better with them caught and behind bars. Oh my gosh! I didn't ask how you are!" She reached out to his face, then stopped herself.

"I've had worse, ma'am." He smiled.

∽

As they approached the school, Mia saw her son standing on the sidewalk next to a man who was holding an umbrella for the both of them. Mia had the door open before Fong made a complete stop. She ran out into the light rain, right to Raphael, and gave him a big hug before he squirmed out.

"This is a school, not a babysitting service," said the man with the umbrella.

"Yes, I know, I'm so sorry about that! I promise it won't happen again."

He grumbled.

"This is Daoming."

"Thank you so much for looking after him, Daoming. I'm Mia—"

But he turned around and walked back inside.

Mia got Raphael and herself back into the car. Raphael noticed, "It's yellow now. And it has a new car smell."

She was just strategizing the best way to explain to her son what happened when Fong started driving again and asked, "How was class?"

"Great! I did just what you said! I walked right into the real school and started kicking a wooden dummy and—what happened to your face?"

"Oh, this? Nothing."

Raphael looked at his mom for an answer.

"Oh, we had a bit of an incident..."

"What's that mean?"

Fong answered plainly, "Some gangsters attacked us."

Mia sighed, having hoped not to say anything that could worry Raphael. But he wasn't worried at all.

He said, "Really? Why?" There was a two-to-one mixture of excitement to fear in his voice.

"To rob us."

"It was terrifying," said Mia, trying to steer her son away from any sense of adventure that Fong inspired, and toward caution. "There were five of them. It was horrible."

"Five? Mr. Fong beat up five people?"

"Well, I didn't beat them all up. I just bought your mom some time to escape."

"Now, Michael, don't sell yourself short. It was incredible what you did. Thank you."

"That's so cool!"

Realizing her mistake, Mia was about to correct him, but Fong did it for her. "It wasn't cool. It wasn't like the movies. I wish it were. In the movies, the good guys always win, but real life isn't like that. It could have gone differently. Luckily, your mom has a few moves of her own."

Mia tried to hide a smile.

"Nuh-uh," said Raphael, and Mia was a little offended.

Fong told the rest of the story. When the story sounded too fun and adventurous, Mia tried to make it sound boring and dangerous. When the story sounded too dangerous, Mia tried to make it sound like everything was just fine. She was elated to see her son so proud of her, but terrified that he might experience anything even one-tenth as dangerous.

CHAPTER TEN

As promised, there were two men dressed like Secret Service agents at the hotel when they arrived. They introduced themselves and assured Mia that she was in good hands. Mr. Fong carried the microwave to her hotel room, promised they could buy a new phone the next day, said good night, and left them.

Mia didn't sleep well that night. She still had too many questions, and the jetlag had her sleep schedule all turned around. Raphael had no trouble falling asleep. She stayed up late on her computer, looking for answers, sometimes to questions she hadn't thought of yet.

She read up on Chinese history. The Cultural Revolution in the 60s. The recent reunification of Hong Kong with the mainland. She read about the Qing Dynasty. The plant. Not seaweed, seepweed. She researched cellphone tracking. She learned more about blocking radio waves.

Tired, frustrated, and a little scared, she looked across the room to the safe in the closet that held their passports. She thought about just taking them, waking up Raphael right now, and just getting out.

A notification on her laptop alerted her that she had a new email. From AliveToDance. She skimmed over the "thank you for using our service, we rely on donations, etc." and went straight to the report. Her heart sank. She hoped she was wrong. The report said that the candy had been laced with warfarin. The email gave some facts about the drug, used to help treat blood clots but very dangerous in high doses. Just one of these would be a lethal dose.

She looked at her backpack. She'd been carrying around deadly candies this whole time. She opened the bag, reached in, took the tin out, and went to the bathroom. Mia was about to pour them into the toilet but stopped herself. "I can't. This is evidence."

She walked back into the main room, sat at her computer, and looked up the phone number for the police. She reached for the hotel phone and put it to her ear. Again, she stopped herself. She thought about the questions Detective Cheung asked and the way she reminded Mia that she was powerless to defend herself legally.

"Fong's right. I can't afford to be naïve."

She sat back down and read the drug analysis again and again. She thought about what she'd seen in the paper about Xiaoli. No husband. No kids. A few acquaintances through work. Hardly anyone to even notice that she didn't exist anymore. No one to remember her. No one to give her justice. No one to give a damn.

THE CAR CAME at 9 a.m. and the Treadwells walked out to be picked up. Mia sat up front with Fong.

"What's the plan today, ma'am?"

"I need a new phone. I don't want to carry a microwave around everywhere I go."

Fong nodded. He drove them into an especially poor area, where the roads became so narrow that they were almost alleys. People walked right through the streets, with no fear of being run over. The going was slow, but Fong parked in the middle of the street and got out, leading Mia into a phone shop. She bought her a new phone with prepaid minutes, nothing fancy. As soon as she removed it from the tamper-proof clamshell package that seemed stronger than the shatter-resistant glass on the car, she could feel how cheap it was just from the weight. Fong found something else to add to her order.

"What's this?"

"It's called a faraday bag. It does what the microwave does, but it's more portable."

It looked like a simple, black cloth envelope with a velcro seal. They went back into the car and Mia exchanged her new "work number" with Raphael and Fong.

"It might not hurt to reset your phone to factory settings," suggested Fong.

"Why?"

"You might have spyware."

"How would...? Of course. Right. Good idea. I'll reset it to remove spyware."

Mia backed up her personal phone on the cloud and reset it to factory settings.

Raphael asked, "Can we get some breakfast before I go to the Shaolin Center?"

"Oh, I don't know if I feel safe with you going there."

"What? Why?"

"Because of what happened yesterday. The attack."

"Ma'am, if you don't mind my saying so..."

"Of course not. You don't need to ask."

"At the school, Raphael will be in the company of several dozen expert fighters. I think the school is as safe a place as can be. Lots of tourists are in there, too, and the police do not want tourists scared off. It's not the kind of place where Triads will mess with anyone, ma'am."

"I don't know." She looked at Raphael. She didn't feel good handing him off to anyone else, but at the same time, she couldn't think of a single reason why Fong was wrong. "Alright. Yeah. That's fine."

They dropped off Raphael at the center, and Mia felt the need to walk in with him this time, just to see for herself. "Call me if you have any problems, okay?"

"I promise."

Mia returned to the car.

"Where to, ma'am?"

"I need to speak to people near Panjin. I'm pretty sure the photo was taken there. I could go myself, but it's an eight-hour flight."

"And it is a bit of a long shot."

Mia looked at the photograph, zeroing in on a young man in the background. "I might have an idea. I need a place to work. Maybe a café or something. What kind of social media is popular in China?"

Fong brought them to a place in Quarry Bay, a spot on the second floor of a café, where they could eat on the roof patio. Mia and Fong sat next to each other. She couldn't speak or read the language, so she needed him to translate everything on her computer screen.

She made an account, uploaded the image of the man in the background, and wrote a fake story about how the man had a distant relative who died and that he, or his family, is entitled to a very nice inheritance if he can be found and his identity confirmed. Mia posted it. Fong ran a business credit card to pay to boost the content, based on location or other demographics. They targeted the boost to people living in Panjin.

They drank their coffees while they waited for the algorithm to do its thing and put that fake story in front of millions of eyes in Liaoning.

"I'm such a bad liar. It's so much easier when I'm typing. What do we say about the inheritance, though?"

"I wouldn't worry about that, ma'am."

"You know what I haven't seen all day?"

"What?"

"Triads."

"I don't understand how Triads would be able to track your phone. That doesn't make sense."

"I don't believe that. I think everything makes sense. It just seems like it doesn't because we're missing some crucial information or we're thinking about it wrong. Everything makes sense. It has to." She reached for her ring finger and started twisting her wedding rings without realizing it.

She looked off the balcony at the cars driving past. At the normalness of everyone else around her. With all the stress since coming to Hong Kong, she couldn't wait to be one of them again. But still... she felt just like she did in Minecart. Finding the box was nearly all she could think about.

Fong responded to an alert on the computer. "Look at that, ma'am—we already have a bunch of hits."

"Already? Do any of them look legit?"

"I can't say yet. Some just ask how much money they'll get. Hmm. Most of these don't look promising. A few people say they think it's their dead grandfather."

"We need to filter them out. What can we add to discourage the fakers or people grasping for straws?"

"How about the name of the village and the year?"

"That might work."

Fong updated the post. He kept an eye on it while Mia ordered another coffee.

"That seemed to weed a few of these out. Several people have already deleted their posts. Hold on, hold on. This one might be something. This guy says he thinks this photo is his father. He doesn't know the exact year, but he says this would be in the mid-to-late 60s, guessing by his dad's age, and would have been in a village called Pudong."

"Is Pudong near Panjin?"

Fong did some quick typing and looked it up. "Very close."

"Ask if we can do a videochat."

Fong typed out the request into a direct message. The computer dinged quickly with a response.

"This guy is in Shandong, but he says his dad still lives in the same village. He's going to call up someone in the village who understands how to work a video chat to help his dad out. Also, he's asking about how much money."

"Just tell him we can't breach the confidentiality agreement until we verify his identity... or something else that sounds legal."

He typed out her thoughts. "He says he's going to make some calls but he should be able to call us in a few hours."

They waited for an hour and a half.

"Hey, Michael. Thanks for saving my life."

"Thanks for saving mine."

"We have some time to kill, so I might as well tell you about why I don't teach now."

"Like I said, ma'am. It's none of my business."

"No, I want to tell you. I want to tell you before you search for it yourself online and get the wrong idea."

He nodded.

"I was teaching at NYU and I wrote a paper. About Adolf Hitler's opinions on art. You probably know this already, but he was rejected from an art school he applied to. He wasn't terrible—as an artist, I mean—if I'm being honest, but he had a lot of difficulty with vanishing points and his style was just a less-impressive version of classics. He wanted to be another Bernardo Bellotto, but he was more like... bargain-brand Bernardo Bellotto. People often joke that if he'd been admitted into art school, World War II never would have happened."

Fong leaned in, interested to hear the story.

"In his totalitarian state, art he disliked was all destroyed. Burned. The Nazis called art that offended their sensibilities degenerate. Some of that art was the kind of stuff produced by graduates of the same school that wouldn't admit Hitler. Abstract art. Modernists. He wanted the artistic taste of Germany to be, coincidentally, exactly his taste in art. And, of course, his taste in art was the kind he tried to replicate. So I had a cheeky theory. Maybe Hitler was primarily motivated by the power to control art. To force people to accept and celebrate the art he loved. To accept and celebrate *his* art."

Fong rubbed his chin. She had his undivided attention.

"And in a perverse way, I think it worked. Hitler's art is very valuable now. It's a paradox. No one had any interest in his paintings until he set the world on fire and killed millions of people. That wasn't what got me in trouble, though. It's the next part. Because I also included an analysis of the Christchurch mass shooting in New Zealand. Do you remember that? Was that in the news here?"

"I don't read the news much, ma'am."

"Okay, well, the details aren't too important for this conversation, but the relevant bit is that this spree-killer made a video of the murder and posted it on the internet. The first of its kind, as far as I know. I mentioned that with the growing popularity of NFT art—that's like, internet art made out of bitcoins or something... to be perfectly honest, I don't really understand how all that works. But it's not important. The important part is that NFT art can't be destroyed. Ever. It's on the internet forever. No government can destroy it. Hitler couldn't destroy it, no matter how degenerate it was."

Mia sighed and took a breath and looked at all the people passing by.

She continued, "I predicted that some psychopath would inevitably commit some horrible atrocity for the sole purpose of using the fame to sell an NFT. Basically, copy what I suspect Hitler did on a subconscious level. Can you imagine what an original copy of Charles Manson's music might go for? That's the example I used in the paper, as it happens. A student read my paper and liked it. He liked it too much. And he did it. He came to school one day and killed twelve people and wounded eight others. Some of them were students in my classes. Some were faculty. He recorded himself doing it and claimed it was his senior thesis. He called it a performance art piece, citing this composer, Karlheinz Stockhausen, who once said that 9/11 was the greatest work of art. The shooter sold the video of the shooting as an NFT." She looked away and her eyes were watering.

"Wow. Forgive me if this is crass, ma'am, but... did anyone buy it?"

She did that half-laugh where it's almost a cry. "Some anonymous buyer purchased it through an online auction for $83,914. That's $6,992 per life he took. He went as far as to include my entire paper inside the metadata. I didn't even know what metadata was until *The New York Times* reported on the shooting. Naturally, people blamed me."

"That's not your fault. You know that, right?"

"No. I don't." She looked far off.

The video chat app alerted them that a call was incoming. Mia accepted the call and Fong moved over so he could see, too. The screen was filled with the face of a girl about Raphael's age, who said something in Mandarin. Mia passed the phone over to Fong and he said a few words of greeting.

The little girl passed the phone to an old man whose face was much too close to the phone so he was distorted like a fisheye lens. He adjusted his glasses. He asked a lot of questions to the young girl, and she helped him.

Fong said a few more words, then let Mia know, "He doesn't really get who we are, so I got him caught up. He's happy to speak with us."

"Great. Um. Where do we start? Ask him why he thinks he's the person in the background of the photo."

Fong relayed the words back and forth. "He says that's the village he lived in his whole life. He remembers that day. The Red Guard came and arrested his neighbors and found a cache of forbidden art. They were humiliated and executed."

"Oh my god. Is that for real?"

"Are you asking me, or him?"

"You."

"Yes."

"Okay, um. I don't know. Send him the full photograph. Ask him what else he remembers about that day."

Fong sent the picture and the girl on the other side received it and showed the man. He nodded and had a lot to say.

"He says you're bringing up some bad memories. Most of those students were from their village. They knew the people they killed personally. He doesn't know the young man with the box; he wasn't local. But he knew the photographer. She was from the village, which made her actions that day all the more tragic."

"What was her name?"

"Her name was Zhang Ya Ying. Very smart. Very devoted. Bad temper. He says she was the worst of them all. The cruelest. She couldn't go back and live in the village again after that. No one trusted her. Everyone resented her. Including me, he said. She went south and started a new life. He says he hasn't seen her since."

"What happened to the box?"

"The young people threw everything in the truck and the one from out of town drove off with it."

"They didn't burn the art in front of him?"

"No, they took it away somewhere."

"Where did they take it?"

"He doesn't know. Beijing, maybe."

"Thank you for your time, sir."

"He's asking about the money again."

"Tell him we have to speak with the lawyers and we'll be in contact."

Fong told them and the girl and old man smiled and waved goodbye before Fong hung up.

"We have a name. Zhang Ya Ying. The photographer."

CHAPTER
ELEVEN

Mia spaced out, staring out the window. The day was getting hotter all the time, and just sitting in the car with the air conditioner blasting full strength felt amazing. She kept putting her hair up. Whenever it loosened, the stray hairs would stick to the back of her neck.

Fong finished up his conversation on the phone and hung up. "I have an address, ma'am."

"That's great! It was taking so long, I was getting worried."

"The guy at the Ministry of Public Security says she did move south, just like the old man said. Her kids moved a lot farther south, all the way here."

"Really? That's so lucky."

"I didn't even tell you the best part. It looks like they moved her down here to live with them."

On the way, Fong's phone rang. He answered it, speaking in Cantonese. It sounded like an argument. Mia could just barely hear a woman's voice. Not angry, but frustrated. Fong finally hung up.

"That didn't sound good."

"It's nothing, ma'am."

"A girlfriend?"

He laughed, "No. No, ma'am. That's my grandmother."

"Really?"

"Yes, ma'am...?" He seemed confused by her reaction.

"No, I think that's just so sweet you talk to your grandmother."

"My father is working in Kenya, leading a project building roads. My mom... she's not around. I'm here, so I have to look after her. That's how we do things. She wouldn't go to Africa. I'm not ordinarily supposed to take personal calls while at work, I hope you don't mind."

"No! Of course not. I think it's lovely that you do that. Family can be tough. I'd love to meet her some time."

Fong couldn't help but smile at that. "She hardly speaks English. She's old school. She doesn't even have a cell phone."

They drove up to the small but relatively nice middle-class apartment complex. It looked like school was just getting out, and children were walking home. Mia remembered when Raphael was that age. She missed it. She missed every age.

Fong found a spot and the two of them walked up a few stairs. They looked at the list of names posted and pressed the corresponding button.

A voice spoke back, "*Ni hao?*"

"Um, hello, is this Mrs. Zhang?"

"Yes?"

"Hi, um, I, uh... I'm here to speak with you... about... stuff." She silently cursed herself.

"What?"

"I said, um, I wanted to speak with you about Panjin."

"You want to speak with my mother-in-law? What's this about?"

"I, uh, wanted to ask her about the, uh..."

Another tenant approached, opened the door, and Fong breezed into the building. Mia followed. The elevator was busted.

"Do any elevators work in this city?" Mia huffed as they went up two flights of stairs.

Fong raised a fist to knock on the door and paused. "Ma'am?"

"Yeah?"

"Please don't lie. You are very bad at it."

"I know."

Fong knocked on the door. A voice on the other side said something in Chinese. Fong raised his voice and the door opened to reveal a chubby, middle-aged woman in sweatpants.

Mia said, "Hi, I was hoping to speak with your mother-in-law."

She stepped aside to let them in. The apartment was small and very messy. Objects were stacked into mindless, disorganized heaps: unopened mail, laundry, and dirty dishes. An orange cat started rubbing up against Fong's leg. The woman pointed to another room and said, "She's in there." She sat back down on the sofa seat and continued watching the television program that the guests had interrupted.

They stepped over clothes and random objects on the floor, trying not to trip on anything. The door was cracked open. Fong knocked but no one answered. He opened the door slowly.

She was there. In her late 70s, huffing oxygen through a mask, sat in a wheelchair, staring at the wall.

"I was right. This did seem too easy. What did you say to get her to open the door?"

"I told her we're police."

Mia whispered, "What? You can't do that!"

"Ma'am?" Fong waved a hand in front of her face. She blinked and came to, greeting them in Chinese.

"Hi! Mrs. Zhang, we were hoping you could answer a few questions."

She smiled. Fong translated. "She said... uh... it's not important. But she's not entirely there."

Mia opened up her bag and retrieved the photo and showed it to her. "Did you take this picture?" She took it and looked it over, smiled, and said something.

"She says... she wants to know if we took that picture."

Mia sighed. Fong repeated the question, more slowly. She looked at it again and nodded.

"Mrs. Zhang, what can you tell us about this photo?"

The old woman took the picture and gingerly pet the young man in the photo. Mia tried another approach. "Do you know him?"

She said, "Xiaoheng."

"What's that mean?"

"It's a name," said Fong. He reached into his pocket and immediately thumbed a text and sent it.

"First name or a last name?"

The old lady pointed at her closet. Mia opened the door a bit. It was tightly packed with boxes, clothing, and other plastic junk. A few things loudly fell out onto the floor. The woman kept pointing as Mia moved her hand from object to object, in a silent game of hotter/colder. Fong continued texting someone. Mia found something: a case for a mahjong set. The old woman nodded and smiled.

"No, Mrs. Zhang, we're not here to play mahjong."

She beckoned Mia closer. Mia kneeled and handed her the set. She opened it, but the case didn't have any tiles in it. It had more photographs, more black and white images of the same day. It captured the whole thing. Photos of the young Red Guard carrying out precious objects. Photos of the people who were hiding them, forced to wear humiliating hats. Photos of others spitting and cursing them. A few more pictures of Xiaoheng, but none where you could see his face. And one picture of Mrs. Zhang, taken by someone else. Just a teenager in pigtails and a uniform. A serious but happy face, and a revolutionary fist raised high.

"Would it be alright if I borrow these?"

Mrs. Zheng just smiled and stared at Mia like there was something behind her. Mia looked. It was just a closet.

She said, "Okay, I'm just going to take these now, okay?" She collected them and added them to the folder in her bag with the first picture. The old lady didn't seem to notice, even as she looked right at Mia.

"Are you done with your text chat?"

"Yes, ma'am."

"I think we're good to go."

The old woman said something in Chinese. Whatever it was, it froze Fong in his tracks.

"What did she say?"

"She said, I'm glad they're dead."

She spoke some more. Fong didn't translate immediately.

"Michael. What did she say?"

The old woman started speaking again and Fong translated as she spoke.

"She says she's proud she killed those reactionaries. She says she wished she could shoot a thousand more. She says her proudest moment was…"

"What?"

"Her proudest moment was killing parents and giving their children to the Revolution, to be raised up by the Revolution."

The old lady's distant, strange smile didn't look charming and helpless now. It looked demonic. But it was the same smile. Mia had to look away. Monsters were real.

Mia walked out and Fong followed her.

The daughter-in-law asked, "Are you going to arrest her?"

"No," said Fong.

"Why not?" she asked, sounding deeply disappointed. "Did she tell you about how she's dating the Minister of Commerce?" She laughed to herself and lit a cigarette.

"Um, no, she did not," Mia laughed along to be polite.

"Next time, ask her about her billionaire boyfriend, Qián Xiaoheng. We should be so damn lucky."

CHAPTER
TWELVE

They left the building. Fong saw something and scowled, rushing to the car. He plucked a parking ticket out from under the windshield wiper. He looked around to see who put it there. Across the street, two officers stepped out of a civilian car and walked across the street. One was dressed in a uniform, and the other was in plainclothes.

"Hey. That's Detective Cheung."

"Mr. Fong. Dr. Treadwell."

Fong crumpled up the ticket and tossed it onto the ground.

"You're under arrest, Mr. Fong."

"Are you joking? You know who my boss is."

Mia added, "Is this really necessary? What's this about?"

"Please turn around, Mr. Fong," ordered the detective.

Fong did as he was told and the man in uniform pressed him against the car and cuffed him.

Fong said, "This isn't going to go well for you, Cheung."

She ignored him. "Now you, Doctor."

"Me? What did I do?"

"Conspiracy to commit a failure to pay a parking ticket."

"Conspiracy to what?"

The uniformed officer turned her around, shoved her against the car, and cuffed her, too.

MIA DIDN'T KNOW her way around Hong Kong very well, but she did know that the car wasn't heading in the right direction. The police station Detective Cheung worked at was close to the shore, but the driver was taking them deeper into the city. Not a few minutes later, the buildings became thinner and the trees became thicker. The landscape became greener, less concrete and glass. The straight angles of the road became curves, and where there had been buildings, now there were steep rocky cliffs. The car wound up the mountainside until there were hardly any other cars on the road.

"This isn't the way to the police station. Where are we going?" asked Mia.

The driver said nothing. The detective said nothing. Mia looked to Fong, who was on the passenger side. He didn't look back at her. He didn't say anything. Mia swallowed hard.

"Hey, Detective? Um, we seem to be back in the same situation we were in before. I need to pick up my son from Karate school and—"

"Stop talking."

"Um. But you said you understand because you have kids—"

The driver and she laughed and exchanged a few words that Mia didn't understand.

Fong explained, "She doesn't have kids."

Mia felt stupid.

The driver said something in Chinese and the detective responded. Fong said something. Mia didn't understand exactly what Detective Cheung said, but she knew it meant something like, "Shut up." The driver spoke again to the detective. She leaned forward, found Mia's bag which she kept by her feet, unzipped it, and dug around in the disorganized mess. She finally found something and passed it to the driver.

"Hey, what is that?" asked Mia.

The driver popped something into his mouth.

"What is that?" Mia asked again, "Officer, did you just eat one of the candies?" but she knew. The smell reached all the way to the back seat. "Sir! You need to listen to me! That candy will kill you if you don't spit it out right now!"

The driver said, "Shut up!" and turned on the radio and cranked the volume. It played a Cantonese cover of Blondie's "Atomic."

Mia yelled at him again, begging him to spit it out, but he just turned up the music so loud she couldn't shout over it. She looked at Fong. He silently mouthed the words, "Be. Quiet."

The sun was shining and the light stung their eyes when it passed through the cracks between the thick jungle. The landscape began to open up and they could see the city around the mountain, like a ring. Mia's ears popped and the loud music didn't help.

She looked at Fong and mouthed, "The candies are poisoned!" He refused to look at her.

She felt the car begin to drift into the median and she could see the detective yell and shake the driver, but could barely hear her over the music. He jostled back awake and swerved back into his lane. The tires squealed and the car rocked from his overcorrection. He finally got the car straight. He apologized and said something about being sleepy all of a sudden.

Mia tried warning him again, " Stop the car and call 999!"

They kept going, winding around the mountain until they had climbed enough that the vegetation thinned and Mia could really see how high up they were. They passed through a visitor parking lot, but there were no cars there, just orange cones and a parked dump truck, and a sign apologizing for the inconvenience while the area was under repair.

She could feel the drift again. The car started veering, the driver's head lolling about, his neck muscles limp. Mia kept shouting, the detective, too. Fong didn't have any fear in his eyes. He contorted his body, slipping his cuffed hands under his rear and then over his feet, so they were in front of him.

The driver went completely limp, his body lazily flopped sideways, over the console, and nearly onto the detective, except for his seatbelt. Cheung grabbed for the steering wheel to get it under control, but it was too late. The car veered over the side of the road, down a steep grassy hill, bouncing out of control as they headed toward the visitor parking lot they'd passed a minute earlier, while the woman on the radio sang the chorus in English, "Take me tooooniiiiight…"

THEY CAME to a violent stop when the car collided with the dump truck. Mia's body and head whipped forward and she lost herself for a moment. The music had stopped, and the radio was damaged. She blinked through the spots in her eyes and saw the driver was completely unconscious. Probably dead.

She checked to see how Fong was doing. His arms were over the seat in front of him, using the cuffs as a garrotte to strangle the detective. His eyes were big, and the choke was so tight that she barely make a choking sound. Fong's knees were pressed up against the back of her seat and his whole upper body was arched back. The muscles in his arms were bulging and sinewy, all rallied to the cause.

"No! Michael! Stop!" Mia was still cuffed, and all she could do was try to shoulder him and hurl her body at him. It wasn't enough. The detective went limp and stopped making those terrible, wet noises, but Fong kept choking until the veins in his arms and neck were huge. Mia got tired of trying to stop him before he got tired of killing the detective.

When he was sure she was dead, he unlooped his cuffs from her neck, reached through the broken window, and opened the door from the outside. He stepped out.

Mia realized she was crying. "Why did you do that, Michael? Why did you do that?"

Fong was limping. He opened the passenger-side door, reached into the car and found the keys to the cuffs on the detective, and used them to release himself. His wrists were bright red and he massaged the blood back into them. He walked around the back and checked the driver's pulse. Then, he opened up Mia's door. When he reached for her, she shuffled across the bench seat to the other side and helped herself out.

"Ma'am, I'm not going to hurt you."

"Why did you do that, Michael?"

"I said before, ma'am. You can't afford to be naïve in Hong Kong."

Mia over the grisly scene. The front end of the car was crushed like a soda can, bits of glass all over the inside. Two dead police, the driver the luckier of them. And Mia realized Fong was right. She said it out loud, as she often did.

"They picked us up the moment we spoke with Zheng. They picked us up in a civilian car. They didn't bother calling dispatch. They drove us into the mountains. They were going to kill us."

"Yes, ma'am."

"Because we were getting close to Qián Xiaoheng."

"It seems so, ma'am."

"Who is he?"

"The Minister of Commerce."

"That's what Zheng said. So maybe she wasn't so crazy, then?"

"I don't believe that they are a couple, ma'am."

"What is so important about this box, Michael? What aren't you telling me?"

He took a step forward. She took two back. He showed his hands as if that would make her feel more secure. He held out the key.

"It's a lot easier if you let me uncuff you, ma'am." He took another step toward her, and once again she took two back. Fong held up the key so she could see it, set it down on the car seat, and stepped back several big steps to give her space.

She came up to the open door, crouched so her hands behind her back could reach, stood up, and uncuffed herself.

"Did you hurt your leg?"

"It's nothing," said Fong. "An old injury from my days doing stunts."

"Who were you texting while I was speaking with Zheng?"

"My grandmother."

Mia's mouth went dry. She swallowed. "If my phone was bugged, maybe yours is, too. Or maybe whoever you sent that message to is." She could see by the look on his face that Fong hadn't considered that.

Mia reached into the passenger seat and took her bag back, dropping the cuffs and keys into it. She double-checked and the tin of poisoned candies was still in there. She picked them up and was about to put them back into her bag but paused and looked up. Fong was looking at her. She put the tin in her bag and slipped her arms through the straps.

She cleared her throat. "Okay, um… so what now?" She tried to look nonchalant. Her eyes moved everywhere except to Fong as if he could know her thoughts by eye contact. "I guess we hike down the mountain?"

Fong didn't answer. His eyes were on her like a spotlight in a prison yard. She faked a little laugh. It came out as awkwardly as she hoped it wouldn't. "What?"

"Do you have something else you'd like to ask me?"

"Nope. Let's start walking." She looked away and headed down the road.

Hearing the trunk pop behind her, she started walking faster. She heard his limping, uneven steps catching up, faster than she knew was comfortable for him. She looked behind her. His leg was ailing him, but he was pushing through the pain and carrying his collapsible baton in his right hand.

"Shit!"

She ran to the side of the road and down a slippery grassy slope about 50 feet until it dropped precipitously back onto the road. The darkness got very bright and loud as a pair of headlights rounded a corner and honked. She backed up against the brick wall supporting erosion; the car swerved. Looking up, she saw Fong sliding down after her. She ran across the street into the jungle on the other side.

There wasn't much daylight left and the thick canopy made the jungle as dark as night. She slid down some mud, tripped on a vine, and tumbled a few feet. She started feeling the whiplash in her neck. She heard what sounded like Fong falling and landing on his bad leg, shouting from the pain. She could just make out his silhouette. He tried getting back up and his bad leg gave out.

Mia slowly and quietly continued down the mountain. The growth grabbed her and tried to stop every step and she now understood why people brought machetes to the jungle. She waited a moment and tried to listen for Fong in case he was still following her, but all she heard was the shrill sounds of the insects and birds. She took out the faraday bag that held her phone and texted Raphael.

Mr. Fong is not a good man. Do not go anywhere near him. Get out of school as soon as you can. Find someplace to hang out. Text me when you get there. DON'T talk to the police. Don't go back to the hotel. I'll explain when I can.

Fong hopped to the curb. He took his phone out of his pocket. There was a big crack in it that wasn't there before. He made a call.

"I need a car."

CHAPTER
THIRTEEN

Hau Junjie had a bit of trouble breathing through his nose from the blood in it and that strange, signature smile he always wore wasn't there anymore. He was breathing heavily, made all the more difficult due to the ropes wrapped around his arms and torso, binding him to the wooden chair. They dug into his bare skin and his sweat made them chafe all the more. His wet hair obscured his sight, and the sweat stung his eyes. The brick room had only one exit through a locked steel door. The only other piece of furniture in the room was a small table with a car battery and a pair of jumper cables.

The door unlocked and a woman stepped in. Her back was upright and she wore the deep green, starch-pressed uniform and hat of a People's Liberation Army officer. She was thin and pretty and wore makeup.

She closed the door behind her and stood close, then leaned in and sniffed him. She spoke in Chinese, "You smell awful. Disgusting." She removed a white glove and slapped him.

"I'll never talk, you bitch."

"We have ways of making you talk…"

"You think that car battery scares me? I've been tortured before."

She removed her other glove and tossed it onto the floor carefully. She sat on his lap and wrapped her legs around him. He struggled against his binding, but it was no use.

As she began to unbutton her outer jacket, she repeated herself in a sultry, suggestive voice. "We have ways of making you…"

The moment came to a stop when some K-pop music started playing. The colonel looked at her prisoner, not sure what to do. He said, "Well? Go get it." He sighed in frustration.

The colonel climbed off her prisoner, picked up the phone, and swiped to answer, ending the musical ringtone. She held it up to Mr. Hau's ear.

He said, "This isn't a good time."

"Mr. Michael Fong is here. He says it's an emergency."

"Bring him in through the back. I'll meet him in the yard." He addressed the colonel. "You can hang up now." She did. "Now, untie me." She did as she was told.

He stood up, stretched a bit, and then slapped her across the face so hard that she fell to the floor. She looked up with scared eyes and tried to make herself look small. He leaned down to be closer to her and said in the clearest tone possible, "I said. Not. In. The. Face. Did I not say that?"

She nodded. "I'm sorry, sir. I just got lost in the role and forgot."

"If you want to make it into the movies, you'll need to be better at receiving direction! When I get back, we're going to do it again, and you're going to get it right!"

She nodded quickly and averted her eyes.

He stepped out of the small torture dungeon through

the large, metal door that only locked from the inside, and up some stairs and through a second, less intimidating door, into a beautiful living room. Thin waterfalls dropped from the ceilings and fell into narrow grates, forming walls of water, like wobbly distorted curtains to separate areas. Complete with white leather sofas, the place was an exact replica of a room Hau had seen in a men's catalog for the ultimate bachelor pad. He pulled a silk robe off of a hook and put it on to conceal his nakedness.

He opened a sliding glass door into a fenced-in garden, full of delicate, rare, and expensive flowers. He put on his perfectly practiced perma-smile again as soon as he stepped outside into the evening air.

Mr. Fong was there. "I'm sorry to bother you at home, sir." He kept eye contact to a minimum, looking down often.

"This is highly inappropriate, Mr. Fong, coming to my home like this."

"I wouldn't do so if it weren't an emergency, sir."

"Go on then."

"Two of Qián's police tried to kill me and Mia. I had to... take decisive steps. I believe that the minister may have us under observation. Speaking to you about this in person seemed the safest thing to do."

"Yes, it is. I appreciate that. But it's best to assume we are under observation at all times, whether or not we have evidence for it."

"And Mia knows about the candies."

"That's unfortunate."

"And she knows that I know about the candies."

Mr. Hau tsked. "I'm very disappointed, Mr. Fong. You said you had this under control."

"I do, sir. This is just a speed bump. There have been some unforeseen incidents."

"That sounds suspiciously like an excuse, Mr. Fong."

"No, sir. I take full responsibility. I can fix this."

"See that you do. And how close is she to finding the box?"

"Very close, sir."

"In that case, perhaps it's best not to kill her until she does."

"I was hoping it wouldn't come to that, sir."

"Mr. Fong, you've used her given name twice now. Have you become emotionally compromised?"

"No, sir. I can still do my job."

"I can find someone else if this is too much for you..."

"No, sir. I'll take care of it."

"Perhaps the son would be a good means of controlling her."

Fong swallowed hard and his eyes darted around. "Maybe I could..."

"No, I think the son is the best method going forward."

"Y-yes, sir." He was shaking a bit.

Hau put a hand on his shoulder. He looked directly at him, but Fong wouldn't look back up. "I remember when we first met. I was producing that Donny Li film. I saw you set on fire and kicked off the side of a building. You fell four stories, landed on a giant, inflatable cushion, and some men hosed you down with fire extinguishers.

"As soon as you took off the helmet, the first thing you said was, 'Was the take good, or should I go again?' I saw that and thought, this is a man who can do anything. And the next thing you did? Right away, you called your grandmother to check in on her and see how she was doing. This is a different kind of man, I thought. Was I wrong?"

"No, sir."

"Business, in the movies or in logistic software, is about relationships. About satisfying needs. I need you to do this for me. And you need me to pay for your grandmother's home and medical care. This is how business works. I am good at reading people, at sizing them up. But I'm not perfect. It would be very disappointing to me if I read you wrong."

Fong looked up. "You did make one error, sir. The fall was five stories, not four."

"Good man." He patted Fong on the shoulder.

"I need one thing from you, sir."

"What's that?"

"Please let Mr. Wang at PayWell know I'm speaking on your behalf."

"You have whatever you need, Mr. Fong."

His man left the garden the way he came in. Hau flipped through the contacts on his phone and found the CEO of PayWell. He texted him to expect a call from his representative.

Hau returned inside, removed his silk robe, and called down to the woman, "We're going to try this again. If you want to make it into my film, you will need to nail this audition. Be very persuasive. And I'll remind you *not* to hit me in the face."

FONG STOPPED AT A CORNER PHARMACY. He went inside and grabbed some over-the-counter pain relief pills and bandaids. As soon as he was out, he ate four pills and applied the bandaid to a cut on his nose. He walked next door to a grocer and purchased a small fish filleting knife, tucking it away in his belt. He made a call.

"This is Fong, calling on behalf of Hau Junjie. Yeah." He waited for the call to be transferred. "Hello, Mr. Wang. Yes. Michael Fong. I'm sorry for the late hour. I need you to do a check on any card activity from a woman. Mia Treadwell. I understand that it's difficult. No. No, you misunderstand me completely. I'm not asking you for a favor. It's not me asking. Hau Junjie is asking. Do you understand?

"You are a mid-sized payment processor. Mr. Hau can take his business elsewhere, if that's what you prefer. Just make it happen. You text me if you see any activity. Thank you for your understanding. Yes, Sesame Road also values the relationship with your company, and we hope to continue our mutually rewarding relationship. Thank you."

He hung up and got back in the car. He fired it up and headed toward the Shaolin Center.

CHAPTER
FOURTEEN

The school was already nearly empty. He peeked out the front window to see if Mr. Fong and his mother were there. They weren't. He looked back at the courtyard and the only person still there was Daoming, who didn't look too happy.

Raphael shrugged and made a face that silently said, "I'm sorry." His phone dinged. Mom. A text message. Raphael's mind started racing, trying to make sense of her message. He looked back out the front window. The yellow car was there.

He hustled across the courtyard and approached Daoming. "Is there a back way out of here?"

He pretended to not see him and said something in Cantonese.

"I know you won't respond to English, but this is an emergency! That guy out there... I don't know exactly, but I can't let him see me."

Daoming's eyebrows scrunched. He looked out the front and saw a man milling about, holding up his hands to the sides of his eyes and looking inside. Daoming walked through the courtyard. Raphael followed him through a door to the interior, through a rec room, through a kitchen, until the man opened a door to an alley for Raphael.

"Thanks, man."

He stepped out into the very narrow alley, just enough room for one person to walk through. There was a brick building above him, the alley essentially a tunnel through the city block. Daoming closed the door behind him. Raphael opened his phone. He opened up a map app and looked around for places he could go.

"A videogame arcade? They still have those?" A quarter-mile away. He texted his mom the GPS location, then started walking down the alley and out the other side. The street was lit up in competing colors of red, yellow, and blue signs, and the headlights of the cars that drove through.

He pulled his baseball cap down to shield his eyes but remembered that he stuck out in Hong Kong even more than in America. Hiding in plain sight wasn't an option. He dipped into a shop that wasn't much more than three-fourths of a square made of plywood on the sidewalk. T-shirts and other clothes hung from hooks, often with strange images familiar in America.

He grabbed the first three things he saw: a hoodie with a famous orange cartoon cat (without the proper license) wearing the yellow Bruce Lee jumpsuit, and the words TIGER STYLE. He grabbed a purple baseball cap with the glittery letters HK, and he grabbed an N95 mask. He ran the credit card his mom gave him for emergencies only. He double-checked the street while the man processed his payment. No sign of a yellow car or Fong. He peeled off his shirt and put on his new outfit that looked nothing like what Fong saw him in that morning.

He quoted Sun Tzu to himself, "All warfare is based on deception."

He also saw some bubblegum and rang that up, too.

IT WAS PAST LATE. Mia's whole body hurt. She'd walked for hours downhill through the jungle, unable to call the police because she couldn't trust them. She couldn't call Fong because he was trying to kill her. And she couldn't call Hau because he might be trying to kill her, too.

Mia wandered back into the outskirts of the city feeling ragged. Her clothes clung to her body, damp with sweat and humidity. She caught her reflection in a window and realized she looked as bad as she felt. She checked her phone again. Her signal was back. A couple texts came in. A location. She looked at her phone's map. It would take two hours to walk all the way there. She loaded up her rideshare app and prayed the company had business in Hong Kong. The app struggled to find her location at first.

"Please please please please…"

Wong Fei Hung will arrive in a red Ford Transit Connect in nine minutes. She laughed and jumped, kissing her phone. "Wong, I love you!"

RAPHAEL FOUND the arcade and headed straight for a pinball machine. The fancy graphics of the other games were more impressive, but he had learned to love the tactile experience of pinball and skeeball back in Coney Island. He kept his head down, stayed with his face in the game, and kept to the back of the place, out of view of the street. Mind his business, chew his gum, and wait. That was the plan.

Even in the deafening volume of the blinking machines competing for quarters, Raphael heard someone yell out. He peeked around some cabinets. Two guys were slowly, methodically, heading down the rows, inspecting everyone there, lifting up their hats, pushing them against walls and looking at their faces, shoving them out of the way when they were done with them. No one fought back. No one defended themselves.

Raphael repeated Sun Tzu to himself. "If equally matched, we can offer battle; if quite unequal in every way, we can flee from him."

He looked around for someplace to go. He headed to the back, keeping his hat over his eyes, trying to hide as much of his face and skin as he could. He walked into the hall where the bathrooms, office, and fire exit were. He could see the back door was open, leading right into an alley. He began to hustle toward it when a man walked in with a neck tattoo of a woman, just like one of the gangsters his mother told him about.

He dipped into the nearest bathroom. It was painted pink. There weren't any urinals. A teenage girl was applying some makeup and didn't seem to notice him. He slipped into a stall and shut the door. He tried to lock it but the lock was broken. He stood on the toilet and held out one hand to stop the stall door from opening on its own.

With his free hand, he texted his mom: "There are some guys here. I think they are looking for me. I'm hiding in the girl's bathroom."

Mia got a text and looked at it. She texted back immediately. "STAY PUT. I'LL BE THERE IN," she checked her app for the remaining drive time, "2 MINUTES." Send. The cab parked in front of the arcade. "Thank you, Wong, you are my hero!" She leaped out of the car with no plan.

She spotted three of the Triad's motorbikes parked right outside. She looked through the door at the front of the arcade and saw they were already inside. She remembered their weapons, remembered how Fong had barely survived a fight with them. This was the moment she'd heard about. The urban legends about mothers who became superhumanly strong just long enough to lift a car off her child, or run into a burning building and hold their breath for three minutes, just long enough to rescue their trapped kid. But she didn't go in. It was suicide. And the bikes were still here. That meant they hadn't found him yet.

She looked around for anything that would give her a clue about what to do. Tourists. People selling junk on the streets. The keys were still in the ignitions. She started saying it before she even really thought about a plan. "Bike rentals! Rent a motorbike! Only $5 an hour! No license necessary!"

The three men stopped and smiled and mumbled something like "Hey!" and kept walking. Another young couple walked by.

"Hey, mister! How would you like to take your lady friend for a ride on one of these?" She patted a motor scooter. It was a complete piece of junk.

"No thanks, lady."

She pointed at a group of young men stumbling from the bar. "Hey, fellas! You look like the type of guys who would love to take one of these babies for a spin!"

"Hell, yeah!" Students from England. By the looks of it,

soccer fans whose team had just won. One of them reached into his pocket and stuffed a wad of cash into her hands.

"All yours for an hour. Have fun, guys."

They climbed on the machines, barely even able to stand, probably their first time on a motorcycle. Mia looked through the arcade window and recognized a couple of the goons from the day before. One of the soccer fans managed to get the engine going and started revving it. He laughed and started leading a song for his favorite football club, and the others sang along.

But one of the Triads heard his engine kick on. He pushed past the gamers, straight toward the front, with a face like he saw a man climbing on his girlfriend. Mia ducked out of the way and pretended to shop at an outdoor vendor selling Chinese kitsch, like golden Buddha statues and small Chinese lamps.

The guy on the bike accelerated too fast. The bike flew out from underneath him and skidded into the street, right in front of a taxi. The driver didn't have time to step on the brake and smashed right into it, splashing plastic pieces into the street. The sportsman was on his back and once he and his buddies realized what had happened, they all laughed. The fun ended when the three local men with long criminal records started shouting curses at them in Cantonese.

Mia slipped inside the arcade just as she heard the sounds of a street fight erupt. She saw a glowing light on the ceiling pointing toward the restrooms. She ran full speed through the arcade as the customers abandoned their games and walked to the front to watch the fight instead. She ran down the back hall and into the ladies' restroom. A young woman was banging on the stall door, demanding that whoever was inside needed to hurry up.

"Raphael, are you here?"

The door opened and the woman backed up, surprised by the sight of a 10-year-old foreign boy.

"Mom!"

Mia grabbed his hand. "We gotta go!"

They went back out and slipped through the alley. When they were two blocks away, she said, "Give me your phone."

He did. She dropped it on the ground and stomped on it.

"Oh, come on! Not again!"

"I'm sorry, honey. I'll get you another one when we get home."

Mia hailed a cab that pulled up and they climbed right in. They could hear sirens heading their way, no doubt to break up the fight that Mia had started.

"Hi, sir. Um. Could you take us to a place that's open late and offers some privacy?"

"Like... Wan Chai?"

"Maybe. What is that?"

"The red light district."

"Absolutely not! Something appropriate for a 10-year old boy!"

Raphael interrupted, "What's a red light district?"

Mia answered, "I'll explain some other time."

"If I still had my phone I could just look it up right now..."

The driver said, "Not a lot of places like that, but... do you like to sing?"

CHAPTER
FIFTEEN

Mia paid the young lady at the counter for a few hours of karaoke. She apologized that the credit card machine was down, but Mia had some cash. The Treadwells were escorted into their private room, with colorful, pulsing LEDs on the walls, a disco ball, a coffee table and ring of couches, and a video projection on the wall of all the song options. Once the door was closed, Mia sat down, removed the photos that Zheng gave her, and spread them out so she could look at them all. She took out her phone and took several pictures of everything she had.

She started an audio recording. "Hi, Aldo. I'm doing a job in Hong Kong and things have gotten... weird. Um, my handler here, Michael Fong, is trying to kill me. There was a detective named Cheung. She tried to kill me. Michael killed her. I think the Minister of Commerce is trying to kill us. And the Triads are trying to kill us. Hau Junjie, the wunderkind entrepreneur from the wealthiest-under-40 lists, might be trying to kill us. I think that about covers everyone trying to kill us."

Mia followed up by sharing everything she knew so far, going over all the details about the job, the box, the candies, and the SIM card.

"I'm telling you all this just in case something happens to us. Okay. Thanks. Talk to you later." She ended the recording and sent him all the information.

Mia placed their phones inside the faraday bag, just to be safe. She stared blankly at the array of black and white photos in front of her. Her head was fuzzy. She was exhausted and underslept.

"Are you okay?" asked Raphael.

"Am I okay? Honey, don't worry about me! Are you okay?"

He nodded, but his eyes were sad.

"You know your dad did this thing... he never wanted anyone to worry about him. He always said he was fine, even when he wasn't. Especially when he wasn't. When I ask if you're okay, I'm really asking. I really do want to know. Okay?"

"Okay."

"Are you okay?"

He shrugged.

"No. Of course you aren't. It's stupid to ask." She tried to hug him but he backed away.

"I'm fine. I don't need a hug."

"Well, I'm not fine and I do need a hug!"

Raphael hesitated and gave her the hug. He finally pulled back when she started petting his hair.

"Okay, no hair petting. I get it. I like your new look, by the way."

"I thought Mr. Fong was one of the good guys."

"I did, too, honey. Listen, I have to do some research. If

you need to lie down and take a nap, you go ahead and do that."

"I'm not tired."

Ten minutes later, Raphael was asleep on the couch. The karaoke machine played Blondie's catalog and the projector played music videos. Mia looked back and forth between her laptop and through the trove of additional photos, all taken the same day as the one Mr. Hau provided her. They all confirmed the story told by the old man from Pudong.

Several young people in Red Guard uniforms, armed with rifles. A line of people on their knees, with pointy cone dunce hats on their heads, and signs hanging from their necks with words Mia didn't know, but an online translator told her: capitalist, traitor, reactionary, fool. There was more art—a lot more art. Tapestries, clothing, ornaments, small sculptures, and trinkets. Fantastically elaborate. She wasn't an expert on these pieces, but Mia could see by the quality that they were once owned by very wealthy people.

"If the box wasn't destroyed, maybe..."

She opened up sales records of Chinese art. She filtered by the same criteria that the professor from HKU told her: late Qing, higher-end valuation. She filtered by the images that appeared on the art: a red-crowned crane, a man standing on a dragon, three women standing in front of a winding river. So much of the art shared the same themes, filters reduced her search from a needle in a hay mountain to a needle in a haystack. She wasn't making any progress. She rubbed her eyes. She lifted the phone on the wall and ordered another coffee and asked them to charge her card again for another hour. The clock on her laptop said it was already 4 a.m.

She tried a different tack, searching by buyer. She typed

Hau Junjie and pressed enter. A lot of sales through auctions. She paused on one, a tapestry. She'd seen it before. She reached for a photo and held it up next to the monitor. No. She'd seen it twice. This was the same tapestry she'd said was her favorite in his collection when she met him. She looked through all his sales, but that was the only piece that matched the collection from Pudong.

"That can't be a coincidence, right?"

She searched through the sales history of that tapestry, taking notes about where each piece was sold, who bought them, and when. But she stopped when she saw the name Qián Xiaoheng. The Minister of Commerce. The start of the chain. No other sales record before that.

She searched by the minister's name and found all of his sales records, going back 50 years. Photo after photo of pieces, mostly in private collections now, that all began with him. No sales records before he brought them to market. She kept checking the black and white photos and found them all. Each item was back in private hands in China. This stream of art came to market starting in 1979. All of them.

But no record of the box.

"What happened in 1979?"

She looked it up and found her answer. A dark history of violence and infighting. Mao died in 1976, the revolutionary who brought communism to China in the ashes of the Japanese invasion in WWII. A man worshiped like a god, the source of the revolutionary furor of the Red Guard. But once he was gone, there was a power struggle.

An economic reformer named Deng Xiaoping had to flee the country during the Cultural Revolution to escape Mao's purges of the ideologically impure. His son was less fortunate. He was captured, tortured, and—Mia learned a new word—"defenestrated," which meant he was thrown out a window. In this man's case, it was four stories up and fatal.

The Cultural Revolution was supposed to purge the Four Olds, but reading all about politics in China during this time, Mia didn't see much difference between the courtly dramas and treachery of the dynastic era and the brave, new socialist experiment. Men assassinating each other, arresting each other, exiling each other, in an all-or-nothing game with lethal consequences. Mao's first successor died in a plane crash as he was fleeing the country after a failed coup against Mao. The next died of cancer. The third took power briefly but was outplayed by Deng, who became the de facto leader in 1978.

Deng changed things. He replaced the policy of destroying the Four Olds with building the Four Modernizations. He opened up the country. He let go of the dream of a command economy that had failed Mao at the cost of 60 million lives.

Just as Deng began liberalizing the economy, Qián appeared from obscurity. He was able to find fantastic, lost art that had vanished during the revolution and bring it back home. Qián had a vast network of contacts to bring a lot of art to market suspiciously quickly.

Mia looked into Qián, the Minister of Commerce. He came up the ranks very quickly as soon as Deng took power. He was also rumored to be a majority shareholder in China's largest logistics firm, New Horizons, which came in at just the right moment to monopolize the market. Mia leaned back.

A knock sounded on the door. A young woman entered and refilled Mia's coffee. Mia thanked her and she left.

"Why kill Xiaoli? Qián didn't find or sell the box. Hau

wants it badly. What is it? Why is this box so damn important? What have I missed?"

She looked at the time. It was already 7 a.m. She'd been researching all through the night.

Using an app on her laptop, she placed a phone call to New Horizons. She was bounced around between departments, with a robot guiding her on a senseless maze trying to discourage her and get her to hang up. She tried saying "operator," "human," "real person," and other phrases, but the robot claimed to not understand those commands. Finally, she started using words she always told her son not to say. The computer immediately put her in contact with a human operator.

"New Horizons, this is Satya, how can I help you?"

"Hi. My name's Mia. I'm a friend of Xiaoli Tao. I just heard what happened to her..."

"I'm so sorry to hear that. Yes, we're all pretty devastated."

"Is there going to be a funeral? I'd like to attend, but I'm afraid I don't know who to reach. Or could you give me an address where I can send flowers?"

"Um, I'm not sure, but I think I can find something. Can you please hold?"

"Sure."

A few minutes later, the operator returned. "Hi, Mia? Yes, so I have her boyfriend's phone number if you would like that."

"Yes! That would be great, thank you so much!"

FONG WOKE up in his car when his phone dinged. He sat up, rubbed his eyes, and looked at his phone. She just got a taxi with an app outside of Star Idol Karaoke. He'd never heard of it. He checked the map app and saw it was a few miles away. He opened a police scanner app, which collected radio signals and streamed them online. He fired the ignition, pulled out of the spot he was parked in, and took off on squealing tires through the airport parking lot.

He slammed to a stop to pay to open the gate. He fed it his ticket and ran his card. It was approved. The gate opened, and the process felt excruciatingly slow. He accelerated onto the adjoining road and barreled toward the location, weaving in and out between the cars that respected the speed limit. He encountered a blockage. Two cars on a two-lane road, side-by-side, going the speed limit.

He rode up to just inches behind them, hoping to bully them out of the way. They didn't seem to notice him. He honked and saw some eyes in the rearview. An old man. Fong kept honking. The driver put one hand out the window and waved him to pass. Which he couldn't. Fong looked at the median. A curb with grass. No cars coming the other way.

He turned his wheel and jumped the curb, hearing and feeling the scrape of the undercarriage, drove over the grass between two palm trees, and landed on the road heading the wrong direction, the shocks bouncing and trying to maintain stability. Another car was heading his way. He put his foot on the pedal, driving directly at them. They flashed their blinkers and honked. The moment Fong passed the old man on the opposite road, he turned back across the median, with the same reckless bounce and scrape, and landed in front of the road blockage.

The road was open and he got to test the acceleration and handling of the car for the first time. Some chatter sounded on the police scanner. Someone had called the police. A brief description of his car and behavior was provided, an officer nearby called in to respond to a drag racer on the highway. Fong pulled off at the next exit and slowed down. On the ordinary streets, the red lights were not on his side.

He peeked into an alley. No lights in there. He pulled into it and opened up. On the other side, he saw his street had a green. He took it. Two blocks and another red. Cut through the alley. As he approached the opposite side, a police car drove past. Fong slowed down. Way down. He exited the alley delicately, silently, then waited patiently behind them at the next red light. When it was green, they went right and he went left. Another block. He double-parked on the opposite side of a rundown mall that cut through the city block. He got out and ran through the crowds shopping at the stands and kiosks.

Fong came out the other side. No car. A sign that said Star Idol Karaoke. This was the place, but no cab. No Mia. No Raphael. Was he early or late? He ducked back into the mall but kept his eyes open. He waited.

CHAPTER
SIXTEEN

The Treadwells were in their cab, just a block away from the karaoke bar, when Fong arrived. They didn't even see him.

The cab took them to the docks as the midday sun cast sparkles on the water. Raphael was still yawning. He didn't get enough sleep. Mia was running on pure adrenaline and had gone all the way from tired to wired. The car drove through the industrial area with the vast warehouses, mazes of shipping containers behind fences, loud diesel-powered trucks, and men in hard hats. The skyline was dominated by cranes.

The taxi dropped them off on a sidewalk, right in front of a restaurant built literally on the water. The Treadwells got out and crossed the wooden bridge from the docks.

Mia approached the hostess and said, "We're meeting someone." The hostess nodded and let her in.

The place was busy. It was right on the water, suspended on a foundation like stilts, and there were no walls, just a floor and a roof. The place was packed with working people on tight bench seating. The Treadwells walked around the place, not knowing who they were meeting. Mia hoped someone would realize who she was.

A hand went up. Mia double-checked he wasn't waving to a server. She approached and sat down across from him and Raphael sat beside her. Two other men were already eating at the same table.

"Ping?"

He nodded.

She gave introductions, but Ping was quick to get to the point. "You said on the phone that Xiaoli was murdered."

"Yes. I'm sorry to tell you, but… yes."

"So who are you? How is it you know but the police don't?"

Mia explained meeting her on the plane and finding the candies in her bag and sending them to the lab for testing. "Xiaoli had blood clots, is that right?"

"Yes."

"And she took a blood thinning medication for that: Warfarin."

He nodded.

"Warfarin is also used as a rat poison. Too much is lethal, but in small amounts it can be therapeutic. Someone poisoned her candies with it. When the police investigated, the lab results came up that she ate too much of a medication she was prescribed. That's not so unusual so they didn't look deeper. Even if they had, they wouldn't have found anything, because Xiaoli dropped her tin of candies into my purse while I was in the restroom."

"Why? Why would she do that? And why you?"

"I think she was supposed to meet me on that flight. I think she was supposed to leave me that tin. I think someone poisoned her to stop that from happening."

"Your story makes no sense." He waved a hand, leaned back in his seat, and looked out over the harbor. Birds perched near the restaurant, looking for their moment to snag any crumbs left by customers.

"I'm still figuring it all out myself. I couldn't find very much on her. Her LinkedIn was out of date."

"She was American. Her parents immigrated when her mom was still pregnant with her. She had family here, grandparents, aunts and uncles and cousins, and they came at least once a year. Here, she was Xiaoli. There, she went by Shelly, because it was easier for Americans to say and read. Maybe that's why you couldn't find her. Anyway, she went to school out there and came here to work. We met at a bar. Do people meet that way anymore? She loved that beer from Thailand, whatever it's called..."

"Singha."

"Right. She had a good job. Not sure what she ever saw in me."

"What did she do?"

"She worked for New Horizons. You know it?"

Mia only knew that the minister was involved with the company. She shook her head.

"Well, everyone around here sure does. They do logistics on the mainland. The top firm over there. When you get big enough in China, the bosses in the government don't like it. Once a company gets big, the government appoints positions to CCP members and puts them inside the company. The place basically turns into a state-run business. And once the government is involved, it becomes a monopoly. The founders and investors find themselves pushed out. It happens all the time."

Mia's eyes drifted to the docks, but she was paying close attention to his words.

"It's good to be big in China, but don't ever get too big. The bosses will just take everything from you. That's how it is at New Horizons. It's a private company, but it's not a private company. Xiaoli's job was going to Washington, D.C. and L.A. and back, trying to talk to your government. Whatever that's called."

"She was a lobbyist?"

"Right. With that company being such a big deal on the mainland, they always had to work on deals with foreign companies and governments."

"You said New Horizons does logistics on the mainland, but everyone here knows them. I thought Sesame Road was the big player in Hong Kong."

He scoffed. "Reunification has shaken things up a bit."

"How do you mean?"

"Hong Kong was British until 1997. Britain signed a 99-year contract with China as a concession for losing the Opium Wars. That's why we're so different, here in Hong Kong, and on the mainland. We've basically been different countries for a hundred years. In '97, that contract ended and Hong Kong was handed back over to China and the CCP."

"So why is this happening now?" asked Mia.

"The government used to keep hands-off. They had a one-nation, two-systems policy. See, Hong Kong was doing great, economically. The mainland, not so much. The CCP didn't want to ruin what made Hong Kong great by importing their policies here. They left us alone. Until recently. The CCP put its eyes on us and decided to get more involved. *One* country, *one* system. Half the people here don't call themselves Chinese. They say they're Hong Kongers."

"Texans are kind of like that, too."

"You probably saw the protests on TV."

"Yeah. It looked pretty crazy."

He unbuttoned the top three on his shirt and opened it to show a nasty scar by his collarbone. "Triads stabbed me on a subway with a screwdriver. They thought I was part of a protest when I was just trying to get to work."

"Why would they do that? What do gangsters care if you're protesting?"

"They're thugs. They're muscle for hire. And who pays better than Beijing?"

"Wait, wait, wait. You're saying the government hired Triads to beat up protesters?"

"Of course! Beijing can't get their hands dirty. They know they're on TV. They know the world is watching. So they uh, what's the word...? Outsource. They hire some criminals to do it for them. They don't want police in uniform doing it, making the government look bad. Everyone here knows, but foreigners don't understand. You look surprised. You don't have something like that in America?"

"I sure hope not."

Ping shrugged and buttoned up his shirt.

Mia said, "I don't understand what that has to do with New Horizons and Sesame Road."

"New Horizons basically had a monopoly on the mainland. Sesame Road..."

Mia finished his sentence. "Had a monopoly in Hong Kong. And now Beijing is integrating Hong Kong."

"This is a problem that's giving me headaches every day. The software isn't compatible."

Mia's eyes got big. "Say that again."

"I said that the software isn't compatible. What's all this have to do with Xiaoli?"

Raphael looked at his mom and saw her eyes darting back and forth, the faraway look as she started connecting dots. "Mom?"

"I think I know who killed Xiaoli. And I think I know why."

CHAPTER
SEVENTEEN

The Treadwells' cab stopped at the roundabout in front of the hotel.

Mia asked the driver, "Can you hold on a minute? I'll pay extra."

The driver agreed.

"Raphael, stay here a second."

Mia stepped out and peeked through the enormous bay windows into the lobby. Those security guys Hau had ordered, the ones who looked like secret service, were still at the hotel. She climbed back into the cab.

"We need to get into our room and get our passports," Mia told her son. She addressed the driver again. "Sir, I have a strange request, but... we're getting out here. Could you drive to Repulse Bay?"

"You want me to take you to Repulse Bay?"

"No. I just want you to drive there after we get out."

"You want me to pick someone up there?"

"No, I don't care what you do when you get there, I just want you to drive out there."

"Why?"

Mia passed him a handful of bills. That seemed like a satisfactory answer.

She reached into her purse, pulling her personal phone and her crappy work phone from out of the faraday bag. She reset the factory settings on her personal one. Then, she removed the SIM card from her work phone and replaced it with Xiaoli's. She rebooted it, turned it off again, and swapped the cards before booting it back up.

"This trick worked in Minecart..."

She dropped the work phone on the cab floor, then she and Raphael got out and the cab drove off. She peeked into the bay windows. One of the security men looked at an alert on his phone. He motioned to the other, and they both stood up and hustled out the front door. They looked around, checked their phones, and jogged into the parking lot.

When they were out of sight, Mia and Raphael went inside and into the elevator and headed up to their floor.

"How did you do that?"

"Remember that lady who died on the airplane? She hid a SIM card in my luggage. When I looked at it, I thought it was blank. It wasn't, though. It had a virus that installed spy software onto my phone. So if I'm right, they're tracking that phone to the other side of the island."

"Whoa. That's smart." Raphael was quiet for a moment as he processed what he just learned. He quoted Sun Tzu, "'The enemy's spies must be sought out, tempted with bribes. Thus they will become converted spies and available for our service.'"

"How did you already memorize all that?"

"Mom?"

"Yes, honey?"

"Are you in the CIA?"

"No."

"But if you were, you couldn't tell me, right?"

"I'm not in the CIA, sweetie."

"Are you in the SVR?"

"I don't know what that is."

BEING PARKED ANYWHERE WAS TORTURE. The car felt like a prison. Once again, Fong was sitting in the driver's seat, waiting for anything. Waiting for a card payment, praying it was close. Waiting for any clue that might indicate where she was. He got an alert on his phone: a text message. Mia had just loaded up her train ticket app.

"She's taking the train. Where from? Where to?" His knee was bouncing. He'd drank too much coffee. "You don't go to the police. You can't trust them. You don't trust Mr. Hau. You don't even know how to reach Qián Xiaoheng. So what do you do, Mia? You want to get out. You want to go home. So... you go to the consulate. You need your passport. You went back to the hotel."

The tires squealed as Fong started driving in the direction of the train station nearest the hotel.

MIA DOWNLOADED the app for the train and preloaded it with money. They got their things, most importantly their passports, and left without checking out. They walked a few blocks, popping into a shopping mall and heading down an escalator that led to the subway station. She used the QR code on her phone to pass the gate. The place was congested with travelers. Mia and Raphael were alert, looking in all directions, the only people who weren't looking at their cellphones.

When they were in the main terminal, Mia looked for a path that would reach the US Consulate. They purchased their tickets, found the platform, and waited in the fog of people.

"Mom?"

Mia had spaced out. She was so tired she could barely think. "What?"

"Why do they have a big glass wall in front of the train tracks?"

"So people don't fall onto the tracks."

But the voice wasn't Mia's.

They were both about to turn and face the voice until he said, "Don't turn around." It was Fong. "I have a knife. Listen. We're going to get in together. Play it cool and I won't have to do anything I don't want to do. I kind of like you guys, so I'd prefer it if you don't put me in an awkward position."

Mia said, "Michael. You don't have to do anything you don't want to."

The train arrived, quick and loud.

Fong gave a half-cocked smile, but his eyes were sad. "That's something only an American would say."

The doors on the opposite side opened and passengers filed out; then they closed and the doors on their side opened. Fong adjusted the weight on his feet and made the tiniest grunt when he leaned on his bad leg. Raphael looked behind him, and Fong saw the disappointment in his eyes.

As Fong pushed them forward, Raphael delivered a downward back kick to Fong's knee, the old injury. Fong cried out and fell. He wasn't lying about the knife. He drew it from his pocket as he tried standing up again. Raphael delivered a jumping stomp onto Fong's bad leg again. He screamed out, dropped the knife, and grabbed at his knee. He could feel that same bothersome spot in his lateral meniscus screaming, a piece of anatomy he didn't know the name of until two years earlier when Donny Li leg-swept him in *Wudang Stone Fist*.

Mia grabbed her son and tried to bring him onto the train with her. But he pushed her off. He wasn't done yet. Mia didn't realize how strong he was until he almost took her off her feet with that push.

Fong smiled through the pain. "Nice, move kid. I think I saw that one in *Enter the Dragon*." Experience had taught him that laughter was the best analgesic.

Raphael saw the knife on the ground. So did Fong. Fong reached for it with his hand as Raphael reached with his foot. Raphael reached it first, sweeping it away onto the train behind him.

People were stepping out of the way, no one understanding what was happening, as the doors began to close.

Mia reached out and stopped the doors, which opened again. Raphael kept kicking Fong. The stunt man was laid on his back, fists and forearms protecting his face and body. Mia grabbed Raphael's arm again and pulled him onto the train, pushing her son to the other side of the car and throwing him a look that said, "Stop." He did.

Mia followed. Just as she crossed the threshold, Fong sprung at her like a coiled snake. He couldn't stand on one leg and was still half on the ground. He failed to grab Mia, but he did get her backpack, which slipped off her shoulder. She held on tightly to the bag full of all the evidence she'd collected and tried yanking it away, nearly dragging him onto the train with them, but he had a strong grip. Raphael picked up the knife. He disobeyed his mom and stabbed at Fong. The stuntman dodged but fell forward; he wasn't done wrestling with the bag, even while he was on the floor.

The doors tried to close, but Fong blocked them. An automated notice rang out through the speakers to clear the doorway. Raphael soccer-kicked him in the face. Fong fell backward, his wrist tangled up in the strap of the backpack. The bag was on the floor by the door, which was finally closing. Mia reached to pick it up, but it zipped on its own to the other side of the door, just as the train began moving. The strap was caught under the door.

They heard shouting, some people yelling. Then, silence fell as the platform vanished and the train entered the darkness of the tunnel. Mia picked up the bag. One of the straps had broken and had Fong's blood on it.

"Oh no!" She covered her mouth with her hands. Everyone on the train was looking at them. One person was recording on his phone.

She looked at her son. He had a faraway look she'd seen before. She'd seen it on a man named Kyle, one of her husband's war buddies from Afghanistan.

"Raphael."

He didn't answer at first.

"Raphael!"

"Hm?" He looked at her like he only just noticed she was in the train.

"Give me the knife."

He looked at it in his hand.

"Raphael. Give me. The. Knife." He did. She took it from him, then started checking him for injuries. "Did he get you? Are you okay?"

Raphael spoke to no one, quoting Sun Tzu. "'The way is to avoid what is strong and to strike at what is weak.'"

That scared Mia most of all.

RAPHAEL WOULDN'T SPEAK the whole ride. When the train exited the tunnel and reached the surface and the sun was shining in again, they arrived at the aboveground station and got off. They hustled across two blocks, dodging cars and people, and when they could see it, Mia's heart sank.

The place was swarming with police.

They turned the corner and stopped running, trying to look as nonchalant as possible as they walked a few more blocks. Finally, Mia sat on the sidewalk and leaned against the wall of a building. Her head hurt. She was exhausted.

"Why didn't we go in?" asked Raphael.

Mia was happy he was speaking again, at least. "Those police were looking for us, honey."

He sat down next to her. "We didn't even do anything wrong."

"I know. It's not fair. But..."

"Life isn't fair. Grownups sure love to say that."

"No, Raphael. No. We hate saying it. We hate saying it more than anything. But we always have to tell kids that because it's one of the most important lessons that they need to learn. It's like... when you were in kindergarten, your dad and I worked so hard to teach you to be kind and courteous, to share, things like that. We taught you to be fair to others. That was easy. Teaching you that others won't be fair back, well, that's harder."

"What're we gonna do?"

"Listen. I think... there's something I need to do. I don't

want to do it, but I think it's our only chance to get out of this."

"What?"

"Did Sun Tzu write anything about making alliances? Like, the enemy of my enemy is my friend?"

He shook his head.

"Maybe Michael was right. What he said in the subway. Maybe thinking that I have a choice is just an American way of thinking. Maybe I'm still learning that life isn't fair, too."

Mia took her personal phone out of the faraday bag. She removed the SIM card, inserted Xiaoli's card, and started it up. She sighed. Without dialing a number, she held the receiver up to her mouth and said, "I know you're listening. I want to work out a deal."

A BLACK LIMO arrived less than 10 minutes later. The Treadwells got in. They were quiet. They looked through the tinted glass at the city, and slowly the area looked more and more familiar until the car finally reached the skyscraper that was the HQ for Sesame Road.

"It's going to be okay, Raphael. I love you. You know that, right?"

"I know."

"I'm sorry I put us through all of this."

"I love you, too. It's not your fault. Even if you are in the CIA."

Mia hugged him as if she'd never do it again. "Be safe. Be smart."

She climbed out of the limo and closed the door. As it drove off, she walked inside and spoke to the man at the counter. "Mr. Hau is expecting me."

She was led to the private glass elevator that took her all the way up to his office, but it didn't scare her this time. She was ushered directly into his private museum. Even after everything that had happened, he still had that same Mona Lisa smile on his face.

"Dr. Treadwell. I'm pleased to see you."

"Hello, Mr. Hau."

"We've had a great deal of difficulty reaching you. Mr. Fong hasn't been returning my calls. How is your investigation coming along?"

"I've finished."

"I'm eager to learn about your findings. Have you found the box?"

"No. But it doesn't matter. That's not why you brought me to Hong Kong. I know you don't really care about the box."

CHAPTER
EIGHTEEN

Mia explained everything:

"Things have changed a lot for Hong Kong and your business. Beijing used to leave you alone and let you run your company, but that's changing. Beijing is taking an active role inside Hong Kong. People in the know understand that your company, Sesame Road, can't compete with New Horizons. I mean, you literally can't compete—they won't let you. They're bidding you out of contracts in Africa for the Belt and Road Initiative. It was not cheap. They'd rather not have to bid at all. Your stock price has been nose-diving. It's unfair. I'd be pretty angry if I were in your spot. You have a great poker face, but it must make you angry, too.

"New Horizons. An old company, a legacy of the Deng era. First in and best dressed, and well established. It's so connected to the CCP that it might as well be a department of the Ministry of Commerce. The head of this company that is poised to take everything from you is Qián Xiaoheng, the largest stakeholder. You might be the bigshot in Hong

Kong, but when the Minister of Commerce wants to replace you, you don't stand a chance.

"You needed Qián gone or controlled. That's why you want the box. You don't care about the box itself. You want the person holding that box in the photo: Qián Xiaoheng. The box is the crime.

"Honestly, I don't know if you care about any of the art in this office at all. You only started collecting this stuff about six months ago. Was it some new investment advice? Did you suddenly fall in love with art? Or did you buy it to create the impression that you are a serious collector?

"The Minister of Commerce was a Red Guard when he was young. But he didn't do what he was supposed to do. He was supposed to destroy art. Instead, he stole it and smuggled it abroad. He rescued it. After the Cultural Revolution, after Mao was gone and Deng Xiaoping was running the show, now the art could come back. He sold all of it to the new elites in China, the new wealth. He made a fortune selling the art right back to the same people who wanted it burned just 10 years earlier.

"Of course, Qián wouldn't say where the art came from. He didn't tell anyone why he seemed to have such a great list of contacts to find all these pieces. And while he made a lot of money selling the art he'd stolen from the fire pits, he made friends with CCP officials and people with money, and he had a little smuggling network to boot. He took all of that and turned it into a real logistics business: New Horizons.

"In the States, we had a guy like that. John F. Kennedy came from a family of bootleggers, making and moving and selling alcohol when it was illegal. Basically, they were like the drug dealers of their time. And when alcohol became legal again, they used their connections and money to become one of the most powerful families in the country.

"You already had some private investigators look into Qián and his past. They were the ones who found the photo taken by Zheng. You were pretty sure the boy in the picture was him, but you couldn't prove it. You just had one senile old woman claiming it was him. That's not enough to take down such an important man. Not yet. You needed more. And, maybe, more importantly, you needed to clean up the investigation. You couldn't be caught spying on a high-ranking member of the CCP. That wouldn't go well for you at all. You needed to launder the investigation. You needed it to look like you had no intention of impugning the character of Qián. That's where I came in.

"As I said, all of the art in this room was purchased within the last six months. I found the records pretty easily. Once you had a substantial collection, searching for one more item doesn't seem so strange. Hiring me, a woman who was on a very large podcast, is crucial. I'm an art expert. I do investigations that take me beyond art. I'm someone that you plausibly could have found with a simple internet search. I'm the perfect person for this job, which is why you offered me crazy money.

"You wanted me to follow the trail where your detectives left off, for me to discover on my own what Qián did. He betrayed The Revolution, rescued art, lied about where it came from, and built a smuggling network that didn't become legit until the 70s. That's not going to be good for his career, especially if it becomes public.

"Then, when it all comes out, you have plausible deniability. Like, "Oops! The American 'accidentally' just uncovered all this dirt on a major official, when all she wanted was to find a box for an art collector." I'm a little bit famous. That's what Xiaoli said. There were good odds I'd be in the public again and that I'd talk about what I found. Then the CCP couldn't ignore it. They couldn't cover it up. They'd have to do something about it. Qián would be unemployed. Or in jail, probably. Maybe worse.

"Xiaoli worked for your competitor, New Horizons. It wasn't an accident that she was on that plane. It wasn't a coincidence that she was seated next to me. She left me with a tin of candies and a SIM card. I didn't realize it at the time, but this is an old trick. If you leave a USB thumb drive with a virus on it, someone is bound to plug it in somewhere. And sometimes they plug it into a gigantic computer network for a major corporation or government. Israel took down Iran's nuclear program by leaving a USB drive with a virus on a table at a restaurant where they knew Iranian nuclear engineers ate.

"Knowing that I'm naturally curious, they knew I would plug it into my phone. And just like that, my phone was infected. Qián's people could track me anywhere I went, see what I was looking at online, and hear everything I said near the microphone. It wasn't hard for Qián's Triad thugs to track me down until I stopped the radio waves. I had to reset to factory settings to get rid of it for certain, but even then, I kept it in a faraday bag just in case.

"This is a big company. Something I learned is that when companies get big, agents of the CCP are placed inside to keep an eye on them. You have some people here at Sesame Road, right? They are government spies within your company, in this very building. It must be maddening. Your chief competitor in the market is the boss at the government agency that is spying on you! That's how they knew you hired me. That's how they knew to send Xiaoli to bug my phone. She was already flying back and forth between Hong Kong and the USA, so it wasn't much trouble to get her close to me on a plane. They knew you were up to something, and they wanted to see and hear everything that I did.

"That's why you poisoned her. I don't know if you knew the details of her mission or not, but that's why you killed her. The candies were a great way to make it look like an accidental overdose. But you didn't plan on her putting those candies into my bag. How could you?

"Cheung intimidated me the first time I was arrested. If you hadn't made a call and gotten us out so fast, I don't know what would've happened. She wasn't happy to have to let us go. Later, she tried to kill us the second we stepped out of Zheng's home. That was the moment when Qián got scared that we were getting too close. He was right to be scared.

"I suspected you were involved with the poisoning when Michael talked a policeman into eating one. He spoke in Chinese so I wouldn't understand. But once I watched him choke Qián's personal police detective, I knew that Michael knew they were poisoned. He wasn't the least bit surprised when the driver started dozing off. How could Michael know those candies were poisoned? The only possible answer is the simple one: He had to be involved. I'm a bad liar. My husband said that was something he always liked about me. Fong knew I was a bad liar. I tried to pretend I didn't know, but he could tell. And he tried to kill me when he knew that I knew.

"When I first came here, I thought maybe the glass elevator was a tactic to intimidate people coming to see you for the first time. It should have told me that you're a bully. That you're psychologically manipulative. But I try to see the best in people. That elevator should have told me everything I needed to know about you. It should have told me to go right back to the airport and fly home without even seeing you.

"There are only two things I don't know. Who poisoned her candies? And why do you have a welt on your face as if someone hit you?"

Mr. Hau waited patiently through Mia's story and when he was certain she was done, he took a moment to choose his words. "The candies were poisoned in L.A. I have a long reach, Dr. Treadwell. I have people everywhere. Distance is no obstacle. I can reach out to Florence. I can reach out to Lake George, New York. I can reach out to Minecart, Colorado."

Mia swallowed hard. Hua's choice of locations wasn't selected at random. "That sounds a lot like a threat."

Hau walked over to a display close to his desk where a Han dynasty Jian sword rested on a display. He ran his finger over the blade as if to test its sharpness.

Mia continued, "Did you know why Qián sent Xiaoli on that airplane?"

"I knew she was there to interfere. The specifics weren't important."

"I think they were, though, Mr. Hau. Very important. If I didn't think specifics were important, we wouldn't be here now."

He nodded at the inescapable logic of her remark.

"Xiaoli was there to hide the SIM card in my bag. It had spyware on it."

"I know that now. Mr. Fong told me. He also told me you got a new phone to avoid being spied on and that you wiped your first phone."

"That's true. I'm sure you are very protective against that sort of thing. You probably assume your phone calls are being monitored. You probably have people sweep your office for bugs. That's why your assistant wouldn't give details over the phone. That's why you gave me barely anything when I came here, including the information you received from the investigators you hired before me."

"You are right. I suspect the most precious resource on Earth is no longer water, oil, minerals, or even people. It's our secrets. I'm certainly not the first tech entrepreneur to learn this."

"Secrets are your line of business, Mr. Hau. Specifics are mine. I know Michael was reporting to you. I know he told you my phone was cleaned. And that's why I used the SIM card again. I reinstalled the virus on my phone before coming here."

For the first time, that strange Mona Lisa smile flattened out. Mia took the phone out of her pocket. "The minister has people listening to me and tracking my every move and internet search, while the virus is installed. He's listening now."

She detected the smallest tremor in his body. Recovering his almost-smile, he corrected his posture and took a deep breath. "Xiaoheng attacked you. He hired those violent gangsters to go after you. He sent his corrupt police to kill you. I never did any of those things to you. But you pick him over me. You come after me."

"The two of you didn't give me a choice! I didn't want to do this! I wanted to find a piece of art. I didn't want to be part of your blackmail scheme or political coup! I'm a widow and single mother with $50,000 in student debt. I don't know anything about politics or espionage. I don't want to know! The two of you and your rivalry caught me in the middle. I didn't want to choose sides, but you both put my son in danger. You both did that, and I had to choose the one who I was safest with. He has the better spy network. He found my son at the arcade and sent those gangsters after him, even after I wiped my phone. You have a long reach, but he has eyes everywhere. I'm sorry. I really am. This was the worst decision I ever had to make. I wanted to leave, but... distance is no obstacle, like you said."

"I understand, Mia. I'm not personally offended. We live in a new age of war—fifth-dimensional warfare, where wars are fought with information and cunning. A new cold war without borders, without armies, without flags. Like all full-scale wars, this one has conscriptions and innocent bystanders. I'm afraid that you and your son were the first and almost became the second. I want you to know that I didn't mean to put you into danger. I just wanted to keep what I built. What I made."

"I know. I wish the people in charge would just sort these things out like grownups."

"I hired you because you are good. Based on Mr. Fong's progress reports, you were on the right track. Worth every penny, I might add. Based on your performance, the private investigation firm I hired is considerably overstaffed and overpaid. Really, all I needed was one of you. I told you I'm in the business of reading people. I'm quite good at it. I have to be. I looked at you and I saw a woman who was in over her head. A naïve woman who has been sheltered in academia. But I was wrong about you. You are not who I thought you were. You are a very dangerous woman, Mia Treadwell."

She began to argue, but he turned around and opened up the sliding glass door, stepping out onto a garden balcony. The sun was just peeking up and the wind whipped his perfect hair into a mess. He started climbing up the barrier.

"No!" Mia ran across the office and out the door, reaching for him. He put one leg over the top and gave her one last look with that strange smile. Only this time, it looked real. He slipped over the barrier before she could get to him.

She didn't look over. She didn't look down. She couldn't.

She slumped down onto the floor. The wind was so strong that it dried her eyes before any tears could fall. She remembered hearing this sound only one other time before, a couple of years ago when Raphael was only eight. He was at school that day when a captain and a chaplain came to her home and notified her of her husband. She remembered the sound of the neighbor's sprinkler. The sound of a pizza delivery car driving past. The sun was shining like any other day. The wind was blowing just the same as the moment before. The sound of the sheer indifference of nature, where no one but Mia even noticed that it was the worst day in the world.

Up on Hau's balcony garden, this day was pretty bad, too.

"I'm coming down now," she said, knowing the phone was still listening.

CHAPTER NINETEEN

When Mia got outside the building, the weight of what happened finally hit her. She realized she was trembling a little, while her body adjusted and let her adrenal gland take a break for the first time in 24 hours. She heard the sound of sirens in the distance, echoing through the streets of Hong Kong, surely on their way to respond to calls of a man who had just tumbled hundreds of feet to his death.

A limo pulled up in front of her, and the door opened. She bent down to peek inside. When she saw her son, she leaped in and gave him a big hug.

"Mom, you're crushing me! Come on!"

It wasn't easy, but she let him go. She closed the door. The driver on the other side of the dark sliding glass window that separated them didn't say a thing. She put on her seatbelt and the car started moving. Raphael opened the minifridge. Mia peeked inside and made herself a highball with seltzer water and a top-shelf Japanese bourbon. It tasted like golden heaven.

The limo moved at a slow pace, which felt strange after all that had happened. They got onto the highway and drove out of the city to the opposite side of the island, heading into an upscale area with well-tended gardens and colonial buildings where the former colonial powers lived well.

They passed through a security gate with a brief nod and pleasant word between the driver and guards, who clearly knew each other. They drove down the slow, winding path into a country club. There weren't any players on the green, but by the main building, many people in fabulous outfits made by well-known and expensive designers were milling around, gathering for something important. The car parked and the driver sent a text message.

"Where are we?" asked Raphael.

"Looks like a party."

They waited a few minutes, then finally Mia knocked on the glass to speak to the driver. He rolled it down. "Yes, ma'am?"

"Are we supposed to get out, or…"

"No, ma'am. Please be patient. The minister will be with you shortly." He put the glass back up.

A moment later, there was a knock on the window and it made Mia jump. "Come in…?"

The door opened and two men climbed in and sat across from the Treadwells. One very tall, very thin man with a bony face and large glasses looked to be about Mia's age. The other man was the opposite: overweight, liver-spotted, balding, and almost 80 years old, with skin like melted wax. She knew him from his photos online. Both were dressed in tuxedos.

"Hello. Minister Qián? I'm Mia Treadwell and this is my son, Raphael."

The thin man spoke, while the old man looked at them with wet eyes, like a fish. He said, "Dr. Treadwell, the minister would like to tell you that he is very sorry for the unpleasantness you've had to endure since coming to Hong Kong, and he hopes you will not hold it against China writ large."

"Um, no. I don't." She wasn't sure if she should address the thin man or the minister.

"With that said, we also appreciate your discretion in this matter, and don't wish to see any further injury come to your family. The minister would also gladly cover whatever money is owed to you from Mr. Hau, plus an additional bonus for your upstanding conduct in protecting matters of national security."

Mia wasn't sure if he was speaking genuinely or as a threat. "No. I mean, yes. I mean, I don't care about politics and I wouldn't want to cause any further injury to anyone. The money isn't as important as my son."

The thin man nodded. The minister finally spoke, slowly and deliberately. "Politics are different here. In America, politics are loud. People shout and argue all the time. In China, politics are quiet. They happen privately. Matters are decided privately. You understand?"

"Yes. I'm in China. I can do things your way."

He smiled a bit and nodded. "As for those pictures..."

Mia took them out of her bag and handed them to the minister. The assistant took them.

The thin man asked, "Have you made any copies?"

"Yes, I did. But I'm not like Hau. I'm not interested in blackmailing you or hurting your position in the government. I don't care about any of that. I just want to go home."

Qián nodded. "In China, leaders of government and industry are punished when they do wrong. Some years ago, the director of the State Food and Drug Administration of the People's Republic of China was executed. That is something Americans don't understand. The enemies of the People are brought to justice in a way that American leaders never are. You have witnessed some of that. In your country, the corrupt stay in charge for decades without consequence. Please understand that I don't say that to disparage you or your home. I say this simply to explain that here, in China, the stakes of politics are far more consequential."

Mia nodded.

"You understand easily. That's something to be very careful with. Jian was right, what he said about you. You are a dangerous woman."

Raphael looked at his mom in awe. Qián reached for the door but Mia interrupted.

"Why did you do it?"

The thin man coughed and started to say something, but the minister silenced him with the slightest gesture from his hand.

Mia finished her thought. "Why did you save the art? At first, I thought maybe you were just a smuggler in it to make money. But I can see you are loyal to the party. You're a true believer. So why did you do it?"

The minister relaxed back into his seat. "I have seen many people die. That's not out of the ordinary for a man my age. But most of them didn't die from old age, as people should. We have a very short time on this earth. The things we make, the things we leave behind, are what makes humans special. A beehive is no different from any other beehive, and it lasts as long as the colony. People make unique things. One-of-a-kind, irreplaceable things, like no other earthly creature can. Marx understood this. We are different from animals. We imagine it and then can make it. You are a historian, yes?"

Mia nodded.

"The Great Wall began far back when the Assyrian, Babylonian, and Egyptian empires were still quarreling with one another. You can't build a new, better world without understanding the past. And you can't understand the past if you discard it. I saw the pyramids with my own eyes, many years ago. It was something special, something photographs can't explain. I marveled at them. But I wasn't persuaded to abandon my convictions in communism to worship the sun god, Ra. You understand."

She nodded again.

"Your hair is very messy," said the minister. He opened the door and stepped out. Mia touched her hair self-consciously.

The thin man added, "The minister is very happy with you, and wants you to know that you have a friend in China if you ever need something that the minister can help with."

Mia ignored the thin man and called after the man who stepped out, "Thank you, Minister."

The thin man added, "The minister must apologize for being so brief. This gala is in his honor and he is already late to give an address." He stepped out and closed the door behind him.

"Can we go home now?" asked Raphael.

"Driver? Can you take us to the airport?"

As the limo started moving, Mia took her phone out of the faraday bag. The moment it caught a signal, it vibrated repeatedly as a flood of messages finally reached their destination. Twenty-two new messages. Nine missed calls. Countless emails.

She thumbed through the list. Half were from Aldo. She listened to the first message. In his Italian accent, he cried, "Mia, please tell me you are okay! I just woke up and saw your message! You need to call me back the second you can!" His following messages were all basically the same, but increasingly upset and loud.

She called him back.

"Mia!"

"Aldo! Hi! I'm so sorry for scaring you. I forgot to call you and I muted my phone and..."

"Are you okay? You are fine?"

"Yes. We're fine."

"Raphael is fine?"

"Yes! We're both just... very tired."

"No one is there making you say that?"

"No!" She almost said, "Don't be silly," but given the information she'd sent Aldo, it wasn't a silly thing to ask. Instead, she said, "I'm sorry if I scared you. We're okay. Really. I needed someone to have everything just in case."

"I'm glad you thought of me, *bellissima*. But I wish you'd stay away from dangerous things."

"You know, as I recall, you had something to do with it..."

"Just something to do with it? How very dare you! I made you, Mia Treadwell!" He said it in a joking tone, though if Mia didn't know him and his humor better, she might have been offended.

She laughed for the first time in a long time. "We're getting close to the airport, so I'm gonna let you go."

"Be safe, *bellissima*. Say hi to Raphael for me. Promise to call me and tell me everything."

"I will. Thanks for being such a good friend, Aldo."

They ended the call.

CHAPTER TWENTY

Mia tried to find the first tickets available. The only remaining seats on the plane were first class and the prices were outrageous. She sighed, bit her lip, and checked her bank account. There were several more zeros than there used to be.

"That can't be right..."

She checked her account history. The last transaction was a very generous deposit from the New Horizons corporation, with the note: "For professional consultation work on art valuation." She almost smiled. The money was a lot, and it would take off a lot of pressure. But accepting it felt like a different kind of pressure. The note should have read hush money if it were honest.

She saw her son, ragged, wearing the silly clothes he'd bought on the street to disguise himself. The tiredness of his eyes. The defeated look, even though they'd won. She bought the tickets.

The plane ride home felt twice as long as the ride to Hong Kong. The Treadwells couldn't wait to have their feet on US soil again. Raphael didn't say much. Mia tried to engage with him, but he didn't want to talk. He didn't want to read his book. He mostly looked out the window at the endless clouds. He slept, too. Mostly he slept.

The most he said was when an old lady who sat close by offered him and Mia a butterscotch candy, and they both said "No!" very quickly and a little too loudly.

Mia couldn't sleep. Her head hurt. Everything hurt. She was too tired to sleep. Too much had happened that she still needed to process. She connected through the plane's Wi-Fi automatically, and her phone started dinging with message alerts. She didn't want to confront the flood of messages she'd received, to answer questions and help anyone else with their needs. But maybe it would be so boring that she could sleep.

Email from: Mom. Subject: Is this you?????????

The body was a link to a news story.

CALL ME AS SOON AS YOU GET THIS. YOUR FATHER IS UPSET. Love, Mom.

She clicked on the link. A brief news story about Hau's abrupt suicide, linked to an original story from Japan. That story was much more complex and included a video.

"Oh no."

The video was cellphone footage in Hong Kong. A man was standing in a very high-end car parked in the middle of the road. The car sped off, and the man fell off and hit the pavement at a bad angle. Mia looked away for a moment. It was too painful. She saw Fong fighting off the gangsters, running up to the car, and pulling her out of the sunroof.

"I look terrible..." Mia observed as, in the video, the two vanished into the alley.

She heard Raphael shift in his seat. She looked at him. He was leaning in to see the fight video. "I... know you liked him," said Mia.

Raphael said, "It's no big deal." He pulled his hat down over his eyes and slouched into a sleeping position.

"You know I abhor violence. I can't even look at it in movies, but... don't blame yourself. You didn't do anything wrong."

"Yes. I did." He quoted Sun Tzu again. "'If you know yourself but not the enemy, for every victory gained you will also suffer a defeat.'"

"Please just talk to me. I want to talk to my son, not Sun Tzu."

He pretended to fall asleep. She struggled not to badger him and went back to the article.

The comments section was flooded with remarks like, "Isn't that the lady from Minecart?" and "I think she's the woman from that podcast," or just, "MIA TREADWELL." Other comments were calling the video a fake or were critiquing Mia's driving and Fong's fighting skills. Some agreed that she looked terrible, but she was quick to defend herself in the comments, "I was being attacked by Triads! It wasn't exactly a salon day!" Send. She immediately regretted hitting enter when she saw the commenters appear ecstatic that she had essentially confirmed her identity.

"No. Oh no. Shit. I don't want to be more famous!"

This was not going to help her sleep. More emails. The job offers started rolling in again, and Alternative Theories podcast was begging her for another interview. There wouldn't be a podcast this time. She couldn't tell anyone about what happened in Hong Kong. She turned off all of her electronics and ordered a highball, only because the airline didn't serve sleeping pills.

Even when they finally got home, it still didn't feel like home. They had just moved in a couple weeks before Mia took the job in Hong Kong, and their things weren't completely unpacked and settled in. They slept a lot when they got to their beds and ate a lot of American food when they woke up.

Something was dogging her. Some loose end she couldn't quite wrap up. She found it in a dream—a dream about the people living on roofs.

Mia woke up in a sweat. She had forgotten someone. She ran to her office, sat at her computer, and started looking online. She did some research based on what Fong had told her, but she didn't have much to go on. It took a few hours, but she pieced together who the old woman was by her name, the neighborhood, and her son in Kenya. She found Michael's grandmother.

Without Michael paying her bills and Mr. Hau dead, who would look after her now? Mia couldn't send money electronically, but she used her bank to create and send her a check, to help pay her bills so she didn't end up on a roof like those other people. It certainly made Mia feel better about taking New Horizons' money. She slept better that night than she had in a long time.

Raphael was on summer break and he hadn't made any friends yet. They worked on putting the house together: unpacking, putting things away, hanging up the prints of Mia's art, and installing a new heavy bag in the garage for Raphael to practice on. How quickly just hanging the art and the photos made it feel like home: "Wanderer Above A Sea of Fog" hung prominently in the living room. A rare print of "Still Life With Hand Grenade," Raphael's favorite, hung in the kitchen over the small table. "The School of Athens" hung in Mia's bedroom, a painting of two Greek philosophers making their case for their own perspective with simple gestures: Plato pointing up and Aristotle gesturing to the earth. That was her husband's favorite.

When the art was all up, Mia felt better. And Raphael seemed better, too. He talked less than he usually did. He joked less than he usually did. But he seemed to be returning to himself, and Mia would blame herself if he never got all the way back. What helped most of all was when she found the news story on Fong.

She read through the story about a fight in the subway, and she let out a slow breath when she saw that Fong was still alive. She'd feared the worst. She knew Raphael assumed the worst. He broke his wrist when Mia's bag caught him; when the train moved, it dragged him a bit and tightened on his arm like a noose, but it ripped. She thought about the irony that Fong wouldn't have made it if Mia's bag wasn't cheap junk made in China. When she told Raphael, he pretended that he didn't care one way or another. But she could see it took a weight off of him. Fong was arrested, but there weren't any follow-up stories about charges.

MIA WAS HAVING her first sip of coffee and looking through emails from new, potential clients. Now she was more discerning. She did more research on them before contacting them. If the money looked too good to be true, it definitely was. Most seemed like they were written by crazy people. A man who believed that he was the illegitimate love child of Roy Lichtenstein and wanted Mia to confirm it. A man in Switzerland who claimed responsibility for stealing Edvard Munch's "The Scream." A woman purporting to be the reincarnation of Sandro Botticelli, professing to have secret knowledge of hidden messages in "The Calumny of Apelles." Someone asserting that Banksy works for Israeli intelligence.

She leaned on her elbows on the kitchen table she was using as a desk. "How do all these people get my email address?" She rubbed her eyes and kept trudging through. A few showed promise.

Stolen property in Millerovo, Russia, dangerously close to the Ukrainian border. A California man with some 8 mm film that he believed was a short film directed by H.R. Giger. Some items recovered from a lost ship that vanished in Lake Superior during the War of 1812.

Spotting the mail carrier leaving her porch through the window, she got up, walked out the front, and said a thank you to the postman. A package wrapped in brown butcher paper, about the size of a minifridge, sat by the door, bearing postage from Beijing. She brought it inside and set it on the kitchen table.

"Is that for me?" asked Raphael.

"No, it's..." Mia turned to face her boy. "Raphael! What happened to your hair?"

"You like it?" He rubbed his sandpaper-rough shaven head.

"Why did you do that? Aww. You have such beautiful hair!"

"I wanted to do something different."

"Are you a Buddhist now? Is this some Kung Fu thing?"

"Wushu, Mom."

"Okay. Well. I'll get used to it, I guess. I'm still in a state of shock. I do have one condition, though."

"What?"

She grabbed him and pulled him in close and started rubbing his head. "You have to let me pet your head anytime I want!"

He laughed and pushed her off. "No deal!" He seemed to be in a good mood today, but Mia still couldn't shake the memory of him on the train after what happened to Fong.

"Daoming likes it."

"Who? The guy from the school?"

"Yeah."

"You're talking to him?"

"Yeah. We text sometimes."

"I thought you said he wouldn't speak to you."

"Not in English. I use a translator to talk to him in Cantonese. He thinks I should study Da Hong Quan. That's flood style."

"Are you learning the language?"

He said something Mia didn't understand.

"What's that mean?"

"A little."

Mia smiled, and the pride on her face made Raphael smile, too. "C'mon. What's in the package?"

She found some scissors and removed the paper, cut the tape, and fished through a ridiculous amount of styrofoam packing peanuts until she found a much smaller plastic-wrapped container. She cut away that, too, and peeled it back.

"Oh. Wow."

"What is it?"

She held it up so he could see closely. "Oh my God!"

A box. Red lacquered wood, with very delicate relief

carvings. Images of people in Manchu clothing. Qing Dynasty, in the early Southern Chan Buddhist style, and a red-crowned crane.

"Is this the box you were looking for?" asked Raphael.

"Yeah. It is. I guess he kept it for himself all these years."

She lifted the lid. Inside was a ladies' comb made of jade. She swallowed hard. She picked it up and examined the delicate intricacy of it.

"Can you imagine the skill required to hew teeth from stone this thin? I wonder what it's worth? No. Forget I said that. I don't ever want to know. I'm keeping this forever. I'm giving it to you when I die. This is a family heirloom starting this minute. I don't think we can even leave this out. I'll need to get a safe. Or a safe deposit box at a bank..."

"I don't know. It kind of seems rude," Raphael said.

"What do you mean? How is this rude? No, this is lovely!"

"He's saying you need to comb your hair."

Made in United States
North Haven, CT
30 December 2024